DWELLERS
OF THE DEEP

By
DON WILCOX

I0541407

ARMCHAIR FICTION
PO Box 4369, Medford, Oregon   97501-0168

STRANGE CREATURES FROM THE DEPTHS...

Bill Pierce and Bea Riley were a renown diving team, known all over the world for their amazing feats from diving boards and waterfalls. But on an ocean cruise one sunny afternoon, Pierce was stunned to see his partner and girlfriend pulled overboard by weird horse-fish creatures. He followed them into the depths below and discovered a strange, secret civilization, known only to a handful of surface people. For this was the world of two different races, the spiny-men and the horse-fish. A world that seemed to hold one certainty for both Bill and Bea—neither one would even return to the surface world alive.

Join "the mad man" Don Wilcox for another excursion into his strange worlds of science fiction escapism...

FOR A COMPLETE SECOND NOVEL, TURN TO PAGE 97

CAST OF CHARACTERS

BILL PIERCE
As a pro diver, he was well aware of most dangers that water could hold, but he had never encountered anything like this.

BEATRICE RILEY
She was Pierce's partner in professional diving. But what was it in her past that led back to the depths of the ocean?

GEORGE VINSON
This posh businessman was as slick and professional as they came. But what was the secret he held under his clothes?

WINDY MUFF
He was just a grizzled old sea-codger at heart, with a penchant for telling tall tales.

YELLOW Z
A ghastly-looking sea-creature with a yellow zigzag pattern on his skin. He could be both your friend and enemy,

MARIBEAU
He was a brilliant scientist, a scientist from the surface world— but did his true sympathies lie with the world of upper men?

THORK
This creature whom Pierce had fought was not just another stone-faced spiny-man, but lieutenant to the king himself.

CHAPTER ONE

BILL PIERCE was hurrying up to the deck to keep a date when the alarm sounded.

"Girl overboard! Girl overboard!"

The whistles blew, the big liner churned waters, and began to circle. It would take several minutes for it to stop. Meanwhile everybody scampered to the rail to look for the girl who had gone over.

"It's your gal friend, Pierce," some fellow passenger yelled.

Bill Pierce tore off his coat, kicked off his shoes, leaped to rail.

The girl was a full hundred and fifty yards away. Her arms were fighting the water frantically. Strange behavior for Beatrice Riley, swimming champion.

Bill dived. In a moment he was skimming through the waves with a powerful stroke.

"Hold on, Bea!"

His cry was probably lost in the clamor. Ringing in his ears were the cynical words of some passenger. "Publicity stunt!"

Bill Pierce didn't believe it. The diving team of Pierce and Riley didn't need publicity, and Bea Riley wasn't one to pull a cheap hoax.

Bill caught sight of her. He was less than fifty feet away. He saw her eyes widened as if in pain. Her arms jerked upward helplessly, she sank down.

With all his championship speed Bill Pierce was too late. Or was he?

"That's the spot!" someone yelled at him from an approaching boat.

He surface dived; combed the waters as far as his keen eyesight would reach.

Moments later he came up. But there was no sign of Beatrice Riley.

Sailors dived from the lifeboat, now, and Bill Pierce, catching half a breath, went down for another search.

He spiraled downward, so deep now that green tropical waters grew black against his wide-open eyes. The hammering pressure of the water pounded at his brain. He was baffled by the strangeness of this occurrence.

Now and again he would catch sight of some vague form sliding past, deep beneath him, only to dart away at his approach.

He bounded to the surface gasping for breath.

"Muff said he saw her," one of the sailors yelled. "He said some kinda fish things had her. They were pullin' her—"

"That sounds like Muff," another sailor growled. "He'd lie to you if your life depended—"

"Which way did he see her?" Pierce snapped.

Someone pointed, and Bill Pierce shot down again.

But when he was forced up he had failed once more.

"Who was it saw her?" he demanded.

"Just some o' Windy Muff's baloney," said a sailor deprecatingly.

"But I did!" a redheaded sailor declared hotly. "I saw a bunch o' fish clap a glass barrel over her—"

The sailors shouted him down. It was no time for any of his wild lies.

"But I *saw* it…" Windy Muff insisted. "Just like I said, the fish had a barrel—"

Pop! Someone slapped him across the mouth, muttering, "Can't you see this fellow's very upset over her? Save your damn jokes for another time."

"But I'm not jokin'—"

THEY cut him off, and one of the sailors explained to Bill Pierce that anything the red-haired Windy Muff said seriously could be taken as a lie right out of thin air.

A whistle from the liner called them back. No more time could be spared on a lost cause. Thirty minutes had been lost.

Pierce tried to plunge again, but the sailors grabbed him and hauled him into the lifeboat...

Back in his stateroom again, as the liner's engines rumbled into full speed, Bill Pierce went through the routine of changing into dry clothes. He moved numbly. The sudden inexplicable tragedy had dulled his senses.

A knock sounded at his door. It was a steward.

"The captain wishes to see you in his office, sir."

"The captain?"

"Can you make it right away, sir?"

"Yes. But first—get a wireless off for me." Bill scribbled a brief message, addressed it to George Vinson in Honolulu. "My friend Vin will find this hard to believe. I can hardly realize it myself."

A moment later Bill Pierce entered the office, dropped into the chair across from the captain's desk and agreed to answer a few questions to the best of his ability.

"I've learned that the girl was *pulled* overboard," said the captain. "Do you have any explanation?"

"Pulled?" Pierce tried to shake the dizziness from his brain. The heavy weight of grief was on him.

"They tell me that a rope—or something resembling a rope—was looped around her arms and waist, and the other end led down to the water."

Bill Pierce gave a bitter snort. "That red-haired sailor is a swift liar, isn't he? Out in the lifeboat he was seeing fish run away with her in a transparent tub."

"Anything that Windy Muff says can be taken with barrels of salt," said the captain. "We've heard too many of his stories. But this rope—well, three passengers saw it."

"They must be mistaken." Pierce clipped his words with temper. "If they're trying to cook up a suicide—"

"Not so fast, Mr. Pierce," the captain cut in with a heavy scowl. "Nobody's trying to cook up anything. We're after the facts. What kind of rope do you think Miss Riley might have used?"

Pierce narrowed his eyes. "Begging your pardon, but I think you're off your nut."

The captain's scowl tightened.

"Maybe I am, Pierce, but I can't ignore the evidence. Three passengers substantially agreed on their stories. Miss Riley was standing at the rail, they said, when they suddenly noticed a cord stretching up from the surface of the water. They saw the loop jerk tight around her shoulders and pull her over the rail into the ocean."

"IT DOESN'T make sense." Pierce paced the floor, snapping his fingers nervously.

"By the time the alarm sounded her arms had evidently fought free of the rope—"

"That proves it was no suicide."

"But the cord evidently caught her feet and a weight pulled her to the bottom."

"*What* weight?" Pierce was angry. "Did anyone *see* a weight? Did anyone see her pull the loop around her arms? Well...what's the answer?"

"We're obscure on those points, Pierce. I've got my men searching for anything that might have been used for a drop-weight."

"Drop-weight, hell. How, in broad daylight, could Beatrice Riley or anyone else drop some object into the ocean without anyone seeing it fall?"

The captain had no ready answer. But he faced Pierce with an accusing look. His suspicions were running rampant.

"Answer me carefully, Pierce," he said. "Did you and Beatrice Riley quarrel last night?"

"Well, I'll be dam—your honor, what's the sense of that question?"

"Calm down, Pierce," said the captain. "What you say is being recorded by my secretary in the next room. I won't pry into your personal affairs any deeper than necessary. But if— as a few passengers have testified, you and Beatrice Riley were arguing—"

"It was nothing serious—just a discussion—"

"You'll be doing yourself a service," said the captain, "if you'll relate to me what you can recall of that discussion. That's the simplest way to clear yourself of any suspicion of murder."

For a moment Bill Pierce was livid, tensing his muscles to hold himself in check.

Then he saw his reflection in a panel mirror, and the fury in his cold eyes rebuked him. An outburst of temper was no way to ward off the captain's suspicions.

Pierce drew a deep breath, sat down, after a moment managed to speak calmly.

"Okay, captain. I'll tell you what we talked about. I might as well. I'd be thinking about it anyhow, now that she's gone... Last night when I met her on the deck I told her I'd just received a radiogram..."

CHAPTER TWO

THAT previous evening when Bill Pierce had received a radiogram he had hurried around the deck to find Beatrice.

She wasn't going to like it, he was sure. The telegram was from his friend George Vinson. Beatrice had no use for Vinson. She held an unaccountable dislike for him.

"Just my luck," Bill Pierce had said to himself.

Bill was madly in love with Beatrice. Her mysterious nature always held him at a distance. But he was determined to slip a ring on her finger before they reached Honolulu.

Now with the Hawaiian Islands less than two days off, this had to happen.

George Vinson had radiographed from Hawaii. He would be there to meet them. Moreover, he wanted to take them on to South America on his yacht.

Bill Pierce knew Bea would never hear to it.

Bill had came upon Beatrice lounging in a deck chair. She was dressed in her sporty blue and white, looking as beautiful as Bill Pierce had ever seen her—and that was saying a lot.

"A surprise radiogram for us, Bea."

"Not from George Vinson?" she asked apprehensively.

"Good old Vin," Bill smiled. "Are you in the mood? There, there, don't frown so. It spoils your pretty face."

He handed her the radiogram and watched her expression as she read it.

The mystery in Beatrice Riley's face was ever present. It was something Bill would dream about at night and read about in the Sunday sports reviews. It was something that everyone remarked about.

Beatrice Riley was a mystery. She was one of those rare persons who never talked about themselves. She had blossomed into a celebrity after a brief round of bathing beauty contests. The reporters, inquiring about as to where she came from, discovered that no one knew—and the girl herself positively refused to talk about her past.

Before Bill met her he was skeptical of the stories of her sensational diving. Some smart promoter must be hoaxing the public, he thought. A *man* might risk his life in a few of those daredevil dives—himself, for example. But he was tops, or darned near it. But no woman would dare—

Then came the momentous sports show that he and Bea Riley were asked to appear in together. And that changed everything. Bill Pierce saw for himself.

Yes, and he came so near to being outclassed that it wasn't funny. Bea Riley could have walked off with the show. But she didn't. She shared honors with him.

That was the beginning of the team of Pierce and Riley, headed straight for international fame. For Bea was everything the reporters had claimed and more.

From the West Coast they had flown the Pacific to appear in expositions in the Philippines and Australia. Now they were sailing back to the States. New York was already building them up for a summer season appearance, only three months away...

BEATRICE reread the radiogram three or four times, then passed it back to Bill without a word. She looked out over the waters pensively.

"You see, Bea," Bill said in the hearty manner of a salesman with a bill of goods to sell, "good old Vinson has worked up some engagements for us down in South America. You know Vin—always looking out for us. He's got business contacts down there, and they're pulling for us—"

"Bill…you're not considering going?"

"Well, it must be a good thing or he wouldn't suggest it. He's going to meet us at Honolulu and take us on to Argentina in his big sea-going yacht."

Bill saw the disapproval cloud Beatrice's face.

"Did you tell him we'd do it?" she asked.

"Certainly not. I always talk these things over with you."

"And then you do what George Vinson wants you to."

Bill's hot temper wasn't good for moments like these, and knew it. He saw red whenever his path was crossed. And counting to ten didn't help.

"Just remember something," he snapped. "Wait for me."

He struck off around the deck. He had to work off steam somehow. Maybe by the time he came back Bea would be reasonable.

But no, she was never reasonable when George Vinson was concerned. Bill couldn't understand it. She was such a swell, fair person to work with in every other way.

Only six months ago Bill had introduced Bea Riley to Vinson. And what a feud he'd started! All the fine things he'd ever said for his old friend had been wasted. Bea Riley had shunned George Vinson like poison.

Vinson had simply thrust his white-gloved fingers through his mane of fine black hair and walked away, ignoring the insulting treatment.

"What in thunder went wrong between those two?" Bill had asked himself after that meeting of six months ago. Then he had tried to apologize to Vinson. Bea Riley, he said, mustn't be misjudged for her seeming coolness. She was a mystery to everyone.

Bill had also apologized to Bea for his old friend's manners. The important little man couldn't help his extreme dignity. His wealth, together with his penchant for profound thought, gave him an air of exaggerated importance.

As for Vinson's strange habit of always wearing white gloves, *indoors as well as out*—well, he must possess scarred and unsightly hands. That was what Bill concluded. And after knowing him for six years Bill took the white gloves to be as much a part of Vin as his face or his pompadour of fine black hair...

Bill returned to Beatrice and she looked up at him with a quick smile.

"What about it, Bea?" he said.

"Whatever you want to do, we'll do," said Beatrice.

"Gee, honey," he caught her in his arms, kissed her. "You know me. What I want is a honeymoon. In Canada, if you say so."

He looked at her steadily. Her eyelids lowered.

"Are you taking me to South America, Bill?" she asked.

"No. I'll wire George Vinson it's off. From this minute on we're independent. How's that?"

Beatrice searched his eyes. "I hope you mean it, Bill."

"I'll send him a radiogram tonight."

"Think it over till morning," said Beatrice. "I want to be sure you don't change your mind... Let me know at lunch..."

CHAPTER THREE

NOW, near mid-afternoon of the day that was to have brought Bill Pierce and Beatrice Riley to a moment of decision, the diving champion sat before the desk of the captain, reciting his story of the previous evening.

"That's about all," Bill said in a low voice. He touched his handkerchief to the corners of his eyes.

"Thank you, Pierce," said the captain.

"If that's all, I'll go," said Bill. "I want to talk with Windy Muff."

The captain sat silently, frowning. "Pierce," he said, "that girl was the most remarkable swimmer and diver I ever saw. I watched the slow motion movie of her incredible waterfall dive from two hundred feet. I saw her start at the top, dive down fifty feet to the first elevated pool, shoot over the edge with the cascade and down another fifty to the second pool, and so on. Four successive dives in one—all in the midst of that roaring artificial waterfall. When I think of that, Pierce, and the long underwater swim she did—"

Bill Pierce slapped his hand on the table. "You're seeing it my way now, Captain. There's a chance she's not drowned. She could fight water for hours. How far off were those volcanic islands when she went over?"

"About eight miles."

"Let me go back, Captain. Give me your launch. And a compass—"

"Could you keep on a course?"

"Let me take a sailor along. Windy Muff. I'll start at once."

"You're taking a big risk. How do you plan on getting back?"

"I've got a friend in Honolulu—George Vinson. He's got a big yacht—"

"Better send him a radiogram at once," said the captain. "If he puts to sea this afternoon he should overtake you by morning. I'll round up Windy Muff for you and check the log."

THERE was not a minute to lose. Miles of waters were piling up for the backtrack cruise.

Bill shot his radiogram off to Vinson. Meanwhile a note came to him from the captain stating that Windy Muff was seen entering Stateroom Number 90, occupied by one Jean Maribeau.

Bill dashed down the corridor, knocked at number 90. He was admitted by a sturdy immaculate little man with a bristling black mustache and a square jaw.

"Pardon me," said Bill. "Is there a sailor here by the name of—"

"Ah, it is the famous Mr. Pierce. We are honored." Jean Maribeau might have been greeting a long lost brother. "Have a chair, Mr. Pierce. Mr. Muff and I have something interesting—"

"I want a quick word with Windy Muff," Bill said bluntly. "I'm starting back in a launch to try to find the girl that fell overboard."

The red-haired sailor looked up from the desk where he had been preoccupied with some pencil sketches. "Not a half bad idea."

"Has Mr. Pierce heard of your remarkable observation, Mr. Muff?" Maribeau asked.

"Uh-huh," said Muff shrugging. "I didn't reckon he was interested."

Bill Pierce was momentarily distracted by walls full of pictures. They reminded him of the physiology charts in a doctor's office: diagrams of circulatory systems, exposed muscles, skeletons. But the subjects were animals rather than men. Odd, nameless animals, as far as Bill could guess. Obviously this Frenchman was a zoologist and a man of learning.

"Mr. Muff has told me," Maribeau volunteered, touching the points of his black mustache, "that he saw some strange fish creatures capture Miss Riley in a sort of glass tub."

"I've got no time to listen," said Bill. "I'm on my way back. Muff, do you want to come?"

Windy Muff turned to Maribeau. "How about it, Doc?"

"I would give ten years of my life," said the scientist, "to possess one single specimen of those unique sea creatures. Could I go too, Mr. Pierce?"

CHAPTER FOUR

A FEW minutes later the three men got into the twin-motored launch and were lowered into the open sea.

While the liner plowed on toward Hawaii, they roared away on the endless backtrack course into the southwestern sun.

Windy Muff held the craft on a dead line.

"Now, Maribeau," said Bill, "what were you saying about Windy's fish story?"

The scientist opened his packet of books and papers.

"Would you like to see a sketch of their footprints, Mr. Pierce?"

"I beg your pardon?" said Bill.

"Would you like to see the footprints of the fish that got her?" Maribeau repeated. "I've made a drawing from the marks that Mr. Muff and I discovered on the side of the ship."

"Footprints *of a fish?*" Bill stammered.

"Fish isn't the proper term, of course," said Maribeau. "Amphibian would be more appropriate—or anuran—though I must confess this creature is difficult to classify, especially upon the meager evidence of a few footprints."

Bill bent over the pencil sketch.

"Maribeau and I spotted it right beneath the rail where she went over," said Windy. "I'll be damned if this ain't one for Ripley."

Bill gaped at the bold outline of a webbed foot.

"Name it and you can have it, Pierce," said Windy Muff.

"I'd call it a mud splatter," Bill grunted, "though it might be taken for the footprint of an oversized duck—or better, a frog—"

"Now you're getting warm," said Maribeau, cocking his head. "As near as I can place it, it's a huge Surinam toad, a species of water and mud creatures found only in Dutch Guiana. They're quite rare, and strange to say they have no tongues. But this fellow is no regular. He's too large. And too far from Guiana. And too much at home in deep water."

The sketch of the foot, Bill noted, fairly filled the sheet of typing paper.

"He climbed the side of the ship," said Windy Muff with the air of having witnessed it.

"With a rope, apparently," the scientist amended. "We found the mark of a wet seaweed rope and a small hook that he had used to pull himself up to the deck where Miss Riley stood."

"It don't make sense, but Maribeau claims he musta crawled up and lassoed her. The slimy devil," said Windy Muff.

"That's our strange verdict," said Maribeau confidently. "And that argues we're on the trail of some monstrosity *with intelligence*. I never saw anything like it."

Bill Pierce was frowning, trying to digest the bizarre evidence.

"Maribeau," he asked sharply. "What do you make of all this? Do you think such creatures could actually imprison a person with ropes and—and *tubs?*"

"I've no right to theorize on the basis of these footprints," said Maribeau, "but I'll go as far as anyone to find out…"

DAWN found Bill and his two companions nearing the area of the volcanic islands. A clear night and a glass-smooth ocean had facilitated their backtracking excursion.

Now Windy Muff stood in the prow sighting the low mountaintops. He passed his field glasses to his companions.

"When those two peaks line up with us," he said, "we'll be right on a dead shot for the spot where she went over. Then it'll be a matter of farther, or closer, the devil knows which."

"We'll have to pull closer," said Bill. "I remember seeing a bit of cliff along the water-line."

"And a heavy black line on the water—at low tide," Windy Muff added. "Ain't that right, Maribeau?"

The French scientist was lost in his books. With the first gray of the morning he had resumed his ardent studies.

"Don't bother him," said Bill.

"It beats me," said Windy, "how a scientist can take an animal's footprint and tell you what the darned thing looks like."

"Did his description agree with what you saw?"

"The truth is," said Windy, "about all I saw was some green blurs. There wasn't time—" Windy looked up. "Ahoy! Look what's comin'."

Bill turned to see the speck of ship on the northeastern horizon.

"That's George Vinson, or I'm a frog's uncle!" Bill leaped up, stripped off his shirt, and began waving it. "Right to us over the blue. He's made excellent speed, believe me."

Maribeau was aroused by Bill's excited talk, and in a moment he and Windy Muff were following Bill's example, waving banners to the distant yacht.

In a short while the trim white craft nosed up within hailing distance of the launch.

Bill looked up at the yacht's prow where the familiar figure of George Vinson stood like a statue against the sky. It was a curious fact, thought Bill, that a man of George Vinson's diminutive stature somehow always gave the impression of being a large powerful person.

Part of it was Vinson's masterful manner. His superior air at this moment, for example, as he unfolded his arms and raised both of them in a sign of greeting, would have nettled Beatrice Riley if she had been here.

As usual, Vinson was bareheaded, and his long black hair blew like a horse's mane in the breeze. As usual, he wore immaculate white from head to foot, including white shoes and white gloves.

"How does it go, my friend?" came the hale greeting of George Vinson.

"Vin, are we ever glad to see you!" Bill shouted.

"Come on up!"

BILL caught the rope that one of Vinson's crew tossed out and tied the launch up against the yacht's gleaming side. He climbed up, scrambling to his feet. George Vinson's hearty handshake was waiting for him.

"It's been many months," said Vinson, smiling majestically. For minutes the two men chatted warmly. Then the smile went out of Vinson's dark gleaming eyes. "Tell me about this this unaccountable happening. Your message was hard to believe. At first I thought—well, never mind—"

"What?"

"No offense, Bill," said Vinson gazing across the waters reflectively, "but my first thought was, Bill and Beatrice are playing a practical joke on me, just to bring me out to meet them. They're anxious to see me, so they've hatched up this hoax—"

"I only wish that were it, Vin," said Bill. "But nothing could be farther from the truth."

"Are you sure she didn't just strike out and swim to yonder island?" Vinson suggested.

"Hell, no, Vin! You're all wrong," Bill answered. The confident calmness of Vinson could be annoying. It was a trait that tended to give the older man a mastery over any situation. It made Bill feel like a hotheaded youth. "Let me explain. She didn't swim away."

"No?" Vinson passed a white glove over his fine flowing black hair.

"She was pulled overboard—there was a rope—and some sort of green sea creature—"

George Vinson's gloved hand froze on the back of his neck. He stared at Bill, then his mystical eyes peered into the sea. The white slits of scars on either side of his neck reddened. He turned sharply to his sailors.

"Bring out the diving suits."

While Bill and one of Vin's sailors changed into the diving outfits, there was a general recounting of all details of Bea's strange departure. Windy Muff and Maribeau climbed aboard the yacht to add their share of the account. Maribeau sketched a webbed foot. Windy stuck to his story that the creatures were green blurs kicking through the water.

And all the while George Vinson stood with hands on hips and head high, like something carved of granite.

"We're a full ten miles from the islands," he said finally. "We'll scout along a trifle closer. Everyone keep a sharp watch on the waters close about."

BILL climbed back into the launch, and Windy and the scientist followed. They swung the launch around to follow in the wake of the yacht. They could see the Napoleon-like figure of Vinson measuring his steps along the deck, and Bill pulled up within voice range. But the only interchange of conversation was a warning from Vinson to keep the diving helmet ready and keep a sharp lookout. Then—

"Look out!" "Watch it, there!" George Vinson and a sailor both shouted at once.

Bill whirled in time to see it happen. A loop of lithe seaweed rope spun out of the water's surface within ten feet of the launch. The loop fell over the head and shoulders of the scientist. The rope tightened with a jerk.

For a split second Maribeau was almost overboard and gone. The rope went taut like an irresistible steel cable and started off with him.

But the scientist's hands and knees hooked the side of the launch, and in the same instant Bill dived to catch his feet. The rope snapped off an arm's length beyond the edge of the boat.

Maribeau shrank back, muttering profanity in a foreign tongue. He jerked the tightly corded seaweed off his shoulders, flung it to the bottom of the boat, and wiped his slime-covered hands on a handkerchief.

"I saw the critters," Bill gasped. "Just as you caught yourself and the rope went tight."

Maribeau's white face nodded. He had evidently seen them too, but just now he was too scared to say so.

"I seen three," said Windy Muff. "But there musta been more, the way they was pullin'. And if that rope hadn't broke—" Windy stopped to scratch his head. "What the devil were those things? They had arms like monkeys and prickly spines like big lizards—"

"I'd give ten years of my life," Maribeau uttered in a scared whisper, "for just one specimen."

"Wonder what they'd pay for one of us," Windy grunted.

Bill closed the diving helmet down over his shoulders and all talk dimmed and melted together like tunnel sounds. The airtight suit was a flimsy affair, unsuitable for extreme depths, and the oxygen supply was meager. But Bill was eager for a look under the surface.

Bill waved a signal to Vinson that he was ready to go over. But again Vinson was shouting something.

Then the sound of a heavy splash seeped into the bell-jar headpiece. Bill turned, saw the agonized fright in Maribeau's face. *Windy Muff was gone!*

Or rather, he was *going*. A seaweed rope was dragging him down. Bill hastily checked the fastenings of his airtight suit and dived.

The force of gravity was with him on his first plunge for depth. He cut down through the water with a powerful stroke. The retreating figure of Windy Muff was a shadowy blur straight ahead of him. Two fleeting spots of light were Windy's bare feet.

And Bill was almost on them. If the fellow would just stop his senseless kicking—

FOR an instant Bill had the sailor by the toe. But the green creatures must have felt the tug. They suddenly jerked Muff away with frantic speed. Bill couldn't match it—not in a bulky diving suit. The shadowy forms pulled out of his reach and were gone.

That would be the last of Windy Muff, thought Bill. By this time the poor fellow must have taken in a lung-full of water. Bill started to climb.

But at that moment he caught sight of a dim yellow circle of light somewhere farther beyond—and below. He plowed toward it. It had all the look of an artificial light. It was incredible.

He was down deep now. In spite of the inflated suit, the water crushed hard against his sides. Gravity was against him, too, and he had to fight water to keep from being buoyed up.

The circle of yellow was expanding into half a globe that streaked the waters with zigzagging spangles. There was activity somewhere in that vicinity. Now the shreds of light were half clouded with a shower of white sand. So this was near the bottom. They must be imprisoning Windy in one of those transparent tubs. But it was all too black for Bill to see. He crept closer.

By this time the dome of light was on a level higher than his eyes. Suddenly he saw the sharp-toothed outlines of a green sea creature, then a second, and a third. They were passing like sentinels around the top of what appeared to be a cylindrical tank. Its vertical walls were solid black, but the light that fountained out of the transparent top gave it form.

A quick movement from one of the green sea creatures warned Bill. They were on the alert. One of them crossed over the light and he caught a perfect picture of it. Its beady little magenta-ringed eyes were darting about, on sharp watch for trouble. The spines over its back were bristling.

What effect, he wondered, would those spines have on a flimsy diving suit like his? Were they fighting spines? A row of them armored the back of each leg, too. They were like elongated fins, or they might have been rows of thin knife-blades connected by webs.

It was hard to tell, under the distorting water, how large these creatures were. But Bill's best guess was that they were three or four feet long. He was certainly not prepared for an encounter with one of them, much less a band that knew how to work together.

He shrank back. His oxygen would soon be gone. If he could retreat undiscovered, enough would be accomplished for the moment. For by this time, he knew, Windy Muff was either drowned or else imprisoned in an upright tank of compressed air. That left Bill free to follow one of two lines of action.

He could swim back to the yacht for a rope to attach to this undersea cylinder. All hands on deck might be able to lift it, and Windy Muff with it. Or, Bill could come back with a fresh supply of oxygen and wait to see what the creatures might do with their prisoner. That would be his cue as to what had happened to Bea.

One of the other of these plans—but he had better have a quick talk with George Vinson first. He started up.

Then as his eyes came on a level with the dome of light he caught sight of the prisoner. It was not Windy Muff. It was Beatrice Riley.

CHAPTER FIVE

AT THE instant all of Bill's neatly built plans toppled into confusion. The waters about him became a chaos of flashing prisms as he automatically fought to stop his upward climb.

The light must have flooded over his helmeted face, for now Bea was looking up at him. There was a flick of smile with her recognition, cut short by an expression of shock.

Under less perilous circumstances Bill would have interpreted that shocked look as embarrassment. Bea could have been no less scantily clothed if she had been in her diving costume. Obviously her fight against being captured had cost her all of her outer garments.

But her shock was plainly one of fear. Her lips were uttering anguished warnings.

"Bill! Be careful!"

At a glance Bill saw that five or six of the green sea creatures were drawing back into a group. Their beady little eyes were staring at him. The bright red lines around their mouths seemed to draw tight, as if in cynical smiles. They were hovering in readiness to attack.

Bill's glance flashed back at Bea. She was trying to shake her head at him. But her actions were obstructed by instruments that Bill had hardly noticed at first. They appeared to be two large electrodes, one fastened to each side of her head.

There was no time to wonder what all of this strange paraphernalia might mean. Already the sea creatures were coming toward him.

They bounced over the light in V formation—five of them. Their necks bowed like the necks of chariot horses. In fact, there was a strange resemblance between their heads and the heads of horses. Their monkey-like arms pawed the water; they reared their spiny backs and plowed straight for Bill's midsection.

Bill flung himself in a quick somersault. The heavy transparent headgear was the least vulnerable part of his costume. He was barely quick enough to take the blow of their attack on his head. Their spines clicked past like a course-toothed saw scraping his diving helmet.

His instincts told him to descend. There was darkness below. The light from overhead would play an advantage to whoever was nearest the bottom.

The green water-horses were right after him. He kicked a spray of white sand at them, then made a hard curved plunge around the base of the upright cylinder.

But they were in their element, swishing through these dark waters. At once they were coming at him from both directions. With savage fury they shot over his arms shearing the sleeves of his diving suit. The waters beat in upon his arms like sledgehammers.

Back the green devils came from all directions. Their spines were steel sharp. He felt one long sweep of saw-tooth points rip the full length of his spine.

That was the last of his diving suit. Its protection was gone. Only the shreds of it clung to his wrists and feet. He kicked out of it.

The pressure flung water up into his face like a blast from a fire hose, and then his helmet bounded off. He was at the mercy of the deep. His eardrums were near to bursting.

HE WAS holding half a breath. But it would never last him till he climbed to the surface. He was too nearly done in with exhaustion. The pain from the gashes and scrapings of spines was like fire. He was losing blood. A faintness was sweeping in on him.

Bill tensed his muscles into steel armor to fight the crushing weight of water. Could he chance the climb to the surface?

The five savage horse-faced creatures were obviously waiting for him to come up into the light again. To rip his body wide open? He could make out their distorted silhouettes at the upper edge of the lighted dome. Their lithe arms were paddling restlessly. They seemed about to plunge again—four of them. But the fifth...

Bill was uncertain whether to trust his eyes. The fifth of the creatures—the large one with yellow Z-shaped streaks on each side of its green sides—seemed to be holding the other four back. A few bold waggles of the creature's head caused the other four to slide back into the darkness. The last Bill could see of them they were swimming away.

Bill's lungs were near to bursting. He saw a leap of the big "Yellow-Z" toward the upper edge of the cylinder.

At once a square of light appeared at Bill's feet. It was a welcome sight—a door at the base of the cylinder. It had slid open, inviting him. Inside there would be compressed air.

He plowed through the foot-square aperture, rose through a series of valves that drew him up automatically. Suddenly the hammering water was gone. Air struck his face.

Air! His breathless gasp resounded in the cylinder like the intake of a gas engine.

Air!

A floor pushed up solid and dry against his feet. Now he could feel the sting of air against his gashed arms and the stripe along his back. It was a welcome sensation, in spite of the light trickles of blood.

Blackness was sweeping in on him.

He was vaguely aware that he was groping at the smooth paneled cylinder walls, that Bea Riley was beside him, that her arms were supporting him.

But the mad exertion had cost him his consciousness. His head lopped against Bea's side, and everything went black.

CHAPTER SIX

BILL scraped his wrists across his face and rubbed an eye open. Colors swam before him in a bleary fog.

He took a long breath. His lips were dry and swollen. He dimly realized he'd been thirsting for more oxygen. The air was stifling. He was still in the big upright cylinder with Beatrice.

Such nightmares! He'd dreamed he was inside an iron lung that had shrunk into a silvered radio tube, Bea was there too, trying to keep him from falling. The dream made her a part of the electrical instrument. Spasms of electricity had been shocking her, so the dream went, until finally her arms had weakened and dropped him. He'd fallen to the floor of the tube and lain there. His blood had seeped away. And Bea was powerless to help him. She was only a part of the radio tube.

The misery of the dream came back to him as he lay coiled on the floor of the tube. But the dream was partly true, he knew.

His back was no longer bleeding, however, and he knew that the scraping he had suffered from the sea creature's fins had not hurt him seriously.

His elbow was pressing against Beatrice's feet. It was a comfort to know she was still there, though she looked very pale and tired.

Again Bill slipped off into troubled sleep, and the same weird nightmare went round and round.

Then a sudden jolting and rocking of his prison floor brought him back to consciousness. The dream vanished.

Bea was still there, with the electrical instruments fastened to the sides of her head.

A panic of terror struck Bill anew. What were those strange electrical instruments? What were they doing to her?

Her eyes were closed. In the ghastly yellow glow she looked deathly.

"Bea! What's happening?" Bill whispered.

Her eyes opened, she reached a hand down to him and helped him to his feet.

"I'm all right, Bill," she said. "Just dozing."

"They're not electrocuting you or anything?"

"Hardly." Beatrice gave him a mysterious little smile.

"I was a sap to faint away," Bill muttered. "We must be nearly out of oxygen. We've got to get out of there before it's too late."

The upright cylinder gave another lurch. Bill's weight struck the wall and the cylinder tottered precariously.

"Where the hell are they taking us?"

"We'd better get down," said Bea. "We're so top-heavy we almost crashed."

"That'd be all right with me—if we could climb past those devilish things—"

"Horse-fish," said Bea.

"Whatever you want to call them," Bill growled. He went down stiffly on his knees. The cylinder coasted along a little more smoothly. And when Beatrice succeeded in unfastening the electrical instruments so she could crouch closer to the floor, the strange undersea prison rolled along as steadily as something on rubber tires.

"We're learning," said Beatrice. "It's better to cooperate with them."

"Cooperate!" Bill barked. "The thing for us to do is get out."

"They'd pounce on us again, Bill, just like before. They're smart."

BILL searched her eyes. Her tone of voice had carried a strong hint of respect for what she had called the "horse-fish." Did she know anything about these wily creatures?

"We've got to make a break," Bill snapped, rising again with hands braced against the walls. "Get your breath. Let's take our chances—"

"Against the open sea, Bill?"

"There's a yacht up above. He's waiting for us."

"Not Vinson?" Bea cried.

His affirmative nod terrorized her.

She sprang up and clutched his arms. Then the vertical walls swayed and fell.

The water valves groaned and one of them sprang slightly open. A flat blade of water dashed in.

"Come on, Bea!" Bill gasped, scrambling to his hands and knees—for the lurch of the tank had thrown the two of them into a heap. "Now's our chance. We're trapped here unless—"

"No, Bill—"

"Don't be afraid. What's the matter?"

"Does Vinson *know* I'm down here?"

"*Why?*"

"Does he?" Beatrice was almost screaming.

"He knows the horse-fish pulled you off the ship. He's *got* to know we're still alive. He has some divers—"

"Look!" Beatrice breathed with relief. "They're setting us upright. We're still safe here."

"I tell you we're getting out of here!" Bill snapped hotly.

"Go back to Vinson if you want to," she said in a chill voice. "But don't tell him I'm here. I'd rather die."

"Bea!"

It was all that Bill could manage to say at the moment. He let his head fall back against the wall. This was more than he could fathom. How could she hold such an abhorrence for George Vinson? Even now in the face of death her mysterious single hatred overshadowed everything else.

Now the righted tank was again riding along the sandy sea bottom taking them to some unknown destination.

"Bea," Bill pleaded, "please tell me what this is all about?"

She nodded slowly and looked into Bill's eyes with confidence.

"You've always said Vinson was a right fellow, Bill. You've called him good—and sincere—and honest—"

"Well?"

"He *is*," she said quietly. "He's all those things and more. *I knew him before you did.*"

"Bea!"

"He's true blue, Bill. That's why I can't face him. *I'm not!*"

"WHAT are you talking about?" Bill swept his hand across his forehead dizzily. "You're true blue, honey. I'd swear it. Hell, what's this all about? It doesn't make sense."

"Don't try to understand, Bill. Just listen to me. I'm not crazy. I know this part of the sea. I even know what these horse-fish are up to. It was just a chance that they took me off the boat instead of someone else. I was horrified when it happened, naturally—on your account. But I can take my chances—"

"You're talking nonsense—"

The valves slid open and a gust of pure fresh air filled the cylinder.

"There's no time to—tell you more," Beatrice whispered. "Take my word for it. If you love me, Bill, don't ask questions now—"

"Do I take you back with me or don't I?"

"You—if you can—*but not Vin!"*

Bill was breathing heavily. He was scarcely aware that the cylinder was gliding along with a low grinding noise like a metal cart over sands. He only knew he was breathing air again, his mind was clearing, he was thinking fast. And his fighting spirit was about to bound out of hand.

"So you've known Vin before." Bill could feel his cheeks redden. "Has he been in love with you…? Is he now…?"

Beatrice glanced sharply toward the cylinder floor as the valves clanked. She whispered, "They're coming after you."

"If I had a knife I'd slit their bellies," he hissed.

"No!" There was more than terror in her whisper. "We're at their mercy—both of us. Watch them, Bill…*study them.*"

"While they rip my back to shreds?"

"When the time is right I'll send you word. Until then—*wait!* That's all I can tell you."

Through the wide-open valves Bill saw the horse-fish beckoning him to come. Only his faith in Beatrice made him obey.

The last of the rectangular doors closed behind him. He was outside the cylinder, breathing the free air of an immense cavern. And in the half-light that sifted down from a lofty ceiling and towering rock walls he glimpsed the strangest city he had ever seen.

CHAPTER SEVEN

THERE was so much movement close about him that he had no time to take in the details of this immense underground world.

He glanced back at the cylinder from which he had just emerged. The twenty-eight or thirty horse-fish surrounding it paid no attention to him. They evidently meant to keep Beatrice imprisoned, for she had not emerged. Now they were pressing levers to lock the valves.

Their cunning hands grappled with the ropes hooked to its sides. It rolled back down the wet tracks with a crunching of metal wheels over wet gravel. Bill drew back out of the way, watched the big instrument move along, silhouetted against the wide cobweb of artificial lights on the nearest wall.

The horse-fish worked together better than any team of circus animals. They worked with intelligence. Every horse-fish knew what he was about. Together they pulled the upright "iron-lung" down the roadway into the water.

This was the path by which it had come in from the sea. The tracks proved that. So did Bill's sharp sense of direction. That big circular steel door half under water must be one of a series of locks that shut out the sea.

For Bill knew that this place was below sea level. He had never ascended, since his dive; moreover the very air pressure on his eardrums argued that this cavern floor was deep.

Beatrice, still imprisoned, was quickly carted away. As she was passing through the circular opening a gush of imprisoned seawater rushed into the narrow channel, sloshing past the cylinder's transparent dome.

Bea looked back to Bill The intent expression, the slight shake of the head, seemed to say, "Don't forget!"

Then, in his final glimpse, of her Bill saw that two horse-fish had climbed up into the cylinder to replace the electrical clamps on her head.

Then she was gone. The swarm of horse-fish kicking along at the sides of the cylinder passed into darkness. The circular steel door closed.

"Well, I'll be damned," Bill said aloud.

"It's got me goin' too, pal," said a voice back of him. It was Windy Muff, sauntering up and planting a lazy elbow on Bill's shoulder.

"I can't figure—" Bill stopped with a gulp. *"Windy!* Where the dickens did you come from?"

"I went to sea in a tub," said Windy with a dry cackle. "They just now took me out of one of those undersea go-carts—only they had to pull me out with ropes."

"I thought you'd be drowned—"

"They pumped life into me—then scared it outa me again. I can't look 'em in the face without turning ten shades of white."

"WINDY, I'm darned glad you're alive!" Bill smiled grimly. "But you know you've fallen into a devil of a mess down here."

"It'd be a heap easier on the nerves to be dead. Was *that* the gal?"

Bill nodded. "Looks like they're taking her back to sea. This strip of water is the slippery slide to the outside world, if my directions are straight."

The dark waters surged at the channel walls and proceeded to drain away through the circular door. Somewhere pumps were working.

"I think you're right," said Windy. "That's the way *we* came through."

"We?"

"The critters got in my go-cart with me to shake the water out of my lungs," Windy explained. "Then they crawled out again to help pull me through the locks. There was a spell of blackness, and when it lifted I was *here.*"

"Here..." Bill echoed glumly. He gazed around. "My great guns, what a cave! A whole underground city."

"Ain't it." Windy Muff sounded a forlorn note. "If I ever get back to tell about this, they'll never believe me."

"Don't worry about ever getting back," said Bill, nudging his companion.

Several horse-fish were watching the two of them from the not-too-friendly distance of about twenty yards. As a matter of fact, the creatures appeared to be *listening*—though Bill had no way of knowing whether this was possible.

One of the six or eight more attentive horse-fish had a familiar look. His green sides were marked with yellow zigzag stripes resembling the letter Z.

"That fellow," Bill whispered to Windy, "came near to ripping my backbone out. We clashed somewhere out there beyond the wall."

"They've got damned dangerous looking spines," Windy muttered. "Hell, he *did* tear up your back a bit. You oughta unroll a yard of tape and pull yourself together. Feel bad?"

"Not now," said Bill. "Seems like it clotted and began healing as soon as I got out of the water. It's very odd." He glanced up at the advancing horse-fish. "Looks like they're gathering in on us."

Like so many loafers and stragglers stopping at a street corner to look at a pair of out-of-town elephants, the horse-fish came closer. From numerous ponds and rivulets and branching caves of the immediate neighborhood they came.

Some seemed reluctant to leave the water, perhaps because of inertia, but they were obviously adapted to land. Once out of water they came striding on their hind legs.

Some came timidly, like so many bashful schoolgirls. Some strutted, like wise old frogs out of a fairy legend, weighted down with burdens of too much knowledge. Some tossed their horse-fish heads high in an attitude of snobbery and sauntered along with their webbed hands on their trim green hips.

But the most business-like specimens marched up boldly, twirling their lithe seaweed ropes.

THESE brisk marchers were creatures of responsibility, there was no doubt about that. Bill thought he detected a superior sharpness in their glassy spines.

"We're in for it," Muff whispered, turning ten shades of white.

"Don't start anything, Windy," Bill mumbled. "I've had a tip."

"Hasn't she got you in enough trouble?"

"Shhhh... They're listening. That 'Yellow-Z' is watching me like a hawk."

Two of the horse-fish advanced boldly, placed slipknotted ropes around the wrists of each man, and led them across the wet gravel beach. Bill thought it best to humor them. He offered no resistance.

"See all that pinkish light way up yonder?" Windy whispered as they plodded along.

"What about it?" Bill asked guardedly.

"Could be daylight," said Windy. "If we'd jerk loose and make a run for it—"

"That's a good two miles away," said Bill, "and we don't know these underground paths. If these horse-fish can run like they can swim we wouldn't get far."

"They're built to swim like fish," Windy whispered.

"And run like horses. Take it easy, Windy."

"Easy! Ugh!" Windy became less guarded in his talk. "My instinct says fight. Tear into 'em with rocks—"

A sharp jerk of the rope on Windy's wrist silenced him. He rolled his eyes toward Bill and whispered cautiously, "Did you see that?"

Bill nodded. "They *heard* you—and *understood.*"

"I don't believe it. I'll prove it to you." Windy ceased his whispering and said in a normal voice. "Bill, in about a minute I'm gonna slice the hearts out of a couple of these green-bellied—"

The rope suddenly pulled so sharply it snapped. For a moment Windy had the wild eye of a bull calf that breaks out of its halter.

Windy might have had a hot inspiration to take flight, but Bill saw the notion cool. The way the spines suddenly bristled over these horse-fish was enough to make anyone think twice. Windy stood calmly while his guardian horse-fish slipped another loop over his wrist. The party moved on.

"Now what do you say?" Bill whispered.

"Nothing out loud," Windy retorted. "Devilishly odd, though… They musta been disturbed by my tone of voice. They didn't understand the words, do you reckon?"

Bill started to answer, but he saw the eyes of one of his captors roll at him curiously. *They were listening.* Bill was sure of it.

"If they hear, it's damned funny they don't talk," Windy said under his breath. "I haven't heard a squeak out of any of 'em."

"I swear I heard some voices in the distance when they first brought me out into the cavern."

"What kind of voices, Bill? Frog croaks—or horse whinny's?"

"Sort of *human* voices, I thought," said Bill, trying to recapture the fleeting impressions of a few minutes before. "Hard to tell, though, with all the echoes floating around through these caverns."

THE party followed a crooked trail along the natural rock wall. They came to a stop at a circular steel door with a white X painted across it.

Two horse-fish opened the door and silently motioned Bill and Windy in. It was a cavern chamber. Low artificial lights were burning. Bill walked in, Windy followed, and the door closed after them.

The room was unoccupied, and that fact was enough to make it inviting. Bill dropped down on the sand floor and sighed, "Home. Don't wake me till breakfast."

"Jail," said Windy. "Don't wake me till the execution... At least we won't have to face those damnable green devils as long as this lasts."

"No?" said Bill. "Take a look at our ocean view."

The room was partly natural cavern formations, partly artificial walls. But across to the right there was a large glass window. Choppy little waves of gray-green water sloshed against the lower half of it. No skies or horizons were visible. This patch of sea was imprisoned within what appeared to be an endless adjoining cavern. Only the plate glass kept it from pouring into Bill and Windy's rocky cell.

A horse-fish was padding gently along the surface of the water—Yellow Z. He came up to the window and pressed his nose against it.

Windy Muff took one look and burst into profanity. He'd never eat or sleep, he declared, if those loathsome critters kept staring at him.

"As long as you haven't any bed or food," Bill chuckled, "you're not losing anything." He rose, sauntered over to the window, gazed out at Yellow-Z. "The fellow's as friendly as a pet dog."

"Yeah?" Windy snorted. "Well, get him to lead us outa here... Ain't he the same one that sliced you down the back?"

"Right...and then protected me from another attack. I can't understand it."

"Sounds screwy, but if you say..." Windy looked down and hesitated. "Bill...Look at these foot tracks..."

Windy pointed to a confusion of marks in the sand. Bill bent over them. They were human foot tracks. The chamber floor was full of them.

"So we aren't the first to drop into this," Bill muttered. "They're old tracks, though. Maybe years old."

"Maybe we'll be old before we get out," Windy rejoined.

Nothing more was said for some time. Bill explored the cavern chamber. His thoughts were in a whirl. Undoubtedly all these mysteries had their secret meanings. Over in one corner was a miniature streetlight—a pink globe mounted on a pair of ebony legs. He had noticed several such lights on their way to this cavern prison room. The underground city he had glimpsed had been dotted with them.

Pink streetlights that stood not more than four feet high... A window opening into another vast cavern half-filled with sea... Human foot tracks all over their prison floor... And somewhere out in the deep waters Beatrice Riley encased in a metal cylinder with an electrical apparatus clamped to her head... And all through the caverns and out in the sea, myriads of horse-fish—strange hybrid creatures that worked like men—and listened to men's talk—but never spoke.

What could it all mean?

BILL paced until he was dripping wet from the humidity within there prison room. His confusions only deepened. Windy Muff had fallen asleep by this time, and somehow that seemed the sensible thing to do.

In one of the natural rock alcoves Bill found a spring of fresh water. He drank his fill, bathed himself. He spliced the scanty shreds of diving suit that clung to his body, managed to convert the torn strips into fairly comfortable trunks. The air was so warm that he felt no need for any more clothing.

Then he nestled down in a bed of fine sand and treated himself to some sleep.

A clank of the chamber door awakened him. He sprang up with a start. His dreams had been beset by dangers, and this sudden intrusion found him alert for an attack.

"Windy, they're coming in. Wake up..."

But Windy was no longer sleeping. Bill's glance swept the room to catch the sailor calmly kneeling beside the ebony legs of the pink light globe. He turned to Bill with a confident wink.

"They're bringing us dinner," said Windy. "Needn't get excited."

"Dinner? How do you know?"

The circular door had opened and now four horse-fish marched in, each bearing a corner of a tray of food. They set the tray down on a flat shelf of rock, turned and went out. In a moment the circular door clanked closed.

Windy Muff sauntered over to the tray, picked up a nicely browned fish and began to eat.

Bill simply glared. "Well, I'll be damned. Are *you* in cahoots with this gang of green bellied monsters too? ...or have they hypnotized you? Don't eat it, you fool. You'll be poisoned."

Windy Muff grinned and went on munching. "Tastes good to me. Better try some."

Bill looked across to the window. Yellow Z was still hovering out there in the water, his red ringed eyes keeping watch.

"You said you wouldn't eat as long as the critters watched you," Bill mocked. "Look at Yellow Z out there. He's got the same stupid grin on his face that you've got.

"Maybe he's had a good dinner too," said Windy. "Join me?"

"No," said Bill. "I'm too smart to take poison."

Then he caught a second whiff of the delicious fried fish. He edged closer, nibbled a sample. It was irresistible. He sat down beside the tray and ate like a horse.

Windy leaned back against a rock, locking his freckled fingers back of his head for a pillow.

"I've discovered something, Bill. Kinda made me feel different toward these beasts."

"Well?"

"Remember what Maribeau said about those foot tracks? They looked like overgrown Surinam toads—"

"But this was the wrong ocean for animals from Dutch Guiana—"

"Remember he mentioned that those toads don't have any tongues…? Well, maybe these critters don't have much in common with the specimens he was talking about, except for their webbed feet and their spiny backs. But I've got it figured out that they also don't have tongues."

"Because they don't talk?" said Bill skeptically.

"Because they *do* talk in a *different way.*"

WINDY rose and walked over to the pink light globe. He knelt beside it, thrust his head between the two ebony posts so that one of his ears rested against each.

"Come try this, Bill, if you ain't afraid of gettin' electrocuted."

Windy drew back to watch Bill with glowing eyes.

The ebony posts were cool against Bill's cheekbones as he wedged his head between them. Whatever the material was, it had enough elasticity to fit snugly against his ears. He listened. At first he heard nothing. Then, a weird flow of communication...*thought-waves.*

"Have you finished dinner yet? We'll come for the tray as soon as you're through... You're prisoners... Don't try to get out... We can be severe if necessary..."

The challenge sent a flash of temper through Bill's swimming brain.

"...No use to fly off the handle... That won't get you anywhere... You wouldn't be the first *upper-world* man we've ripped to shreds... We turn loose on upper-world men as quick as we do on *spiny-men*... So my words have you guessing, have they? You haven't heard of *spiny-men?* Take a look across the river to the other city... But don't get too many ideas about exploring around... You're staying right here as long as we need you..."

Bill jerked his head out of the weird telephone. He suddenly realized he was breathing hard and his fingers were quivering.

"Didja hear voices?" Windy asked eagerly.

Bill nodded uncertainly. "I got a message, all right—a long, rambling one. But I didn't *hear* a thing."

"Different, ain't it?" Windy's grin froze in an expression of puzzlement. "The first time I listened in I wanted to tear those poles out by the roots and beat myself over the head. I thought I was goin' nuts, hearin' things *that couldn't be heard.* Then I thought how gawdawful hungry I was, and they picked it up."

"How'd you happen to try in the first place?"

"Saw some horse-fish doin' it. Back along our inside wall I found a little barred window that gives a squint of the city. Or rather, both cities—one in each side of the cavern."

"My message," said Bill, "mentioned the *other* city. And there was a lot of talk about *spiny-men*. What the devil are they?"

"Never heard of them," Windy replied.

"The uncanny thing, though," said Bill, eyeing the pink light globe suspiciously, "was the way that voice—only it wasn't a voice—kept answering me. The instant I thought of a question, it answered."

Windy waved his hands helplessly. "Don't be askin' me how."

Bill began pacing again.

Windy chuckled mirthlessly. "Now I know what made the foot-tracks all over this place. Whoever was penned up in this joint last went nuts tryin' to dope out that noiseless phone."

"Listen, Windy," said Bill sharply. "You watched me while I was getting that message a moment ago. Did I talk any—out loud, I mean?"

"Not a word," said Windy.

"Then how the devil could that horse-fish chop me off with an answer every time I *thought* of a question?"

"And how could he talk back to you without a tongue?" Windy shrugged. "Didn't I tell you they've got a different way of talkin'? This is it. Come back to the barred window and you can see 'em headin' into phone booths all over town."

BUT at that instant a flash of green outside the big glass window stopped bill in his tracks. Yellow Z had suddenly fled the waters.

"Musta forgot an appointment," Windy cracked.

Then came wild splashing over the water's surface. It was a chase. A bronze body swam past so close that his elbow bumped the plate glass. Bill caught sight of a coarse-featured masculine face. The man shot on, swimming fast.

Close on his heels came five horse-fish. Their little red-lined faces were blazing with fury. Their red slits of gills were working hard. Their steely spines bristled with readiness to slice flesh and bones.

Water splashed to the top of the window, blurred Bill's vision. As the glass cleared he saw the chase turn into a deadly fight.

The bronzed man whirled with the alacrity of a fish, his long black hair slapped over his shoulder, his wide flat hands jerked a short thin knife out of his belt. His back lurched up out of the water just before he struck.

In that instant Bill caught sight of the row of sharp points—a dozen or more of them—that lined the fellow's back bone.

"If we could bust that window," Windy yelled, "we might save that man's life."

"No." Bill's jaw was set hard. "It's their battle. Besides, he's not a man. He's a spiny-man."

CHAPTER EIGHT

"WHATEVER he is," Windy gasped, "he's picked suicide, swimmin' in amongst those damned green-bellied rippers."

"Maybe so. I don't know—" Bill's unconscious words gave way to breathless silence. He and Windy both pressed their faces against the plate glass.

That knife in the webbed fingers of the spiny-man was cutting arcs into the water like a windmill wheel with one blade. A splash of red leaped up from the waves. One of the horse-fish plowed off from the rest of the party, kicking around in a circle of its own, dragging a black mass of spilling entrails behind it.

Then, ceasing to kick, the knifed horse-fish hung limply in the waves, only five or six feet beyond the window. The waters around it grew discolored, and the red shroud hid it from view.

"Goodbye, spiny-man!" Windy barked, pointing back to the fight.

Bill saw. The largest of the attacking horse-fish—a creature with a ring of black circling the white dot on his side—leaped clear of the water, clear of the spiny-man's head. Simultaneously he whirled belly-up, caught the spiny-man between the shoulders as he shot back to the water. In that split second the horse-fish spines did their damage. They scraped an ugly red line straight down the spiny-man's horny backbone.

"A question of who's the toughest," Windy muttered. "Only there's no question about it. That gash'll lay the fellow low. All they've got to do now is rip his guts out."

"Watch, Windy!" Bill fairly shrieked. "There's the thing I was telling you—"

The fight was suddenly over. The big horse-fish that had taken the back-to-back slide *stopped* it. He gave an imperious waggle with his head and the three remaining horse-fish shrank back. When one of them threatened to attack again he darted challengingly. All three of his companions were bluffed out. It was obvious, Bill noted, that these horse-fish held a healthy respect for each other's spines, no matter how much they disagreed on their motives.

"I don't get it," said Windy Muff blankly, as he watched the hard-faced spiny-man swim off to safety. "That big fellow with the bull's-eye markings on his sides turned into a friend awful sudden-like."

"That's the very way Yellow Z did when he was fighting me," said Bill. "At the very moment he had me down and could have killed me, he went softhearted and called the other horse-fish creatures off."

"I don't get it," Windy repeated.

"I don't either," Bill admitted. He lingered at the window until "Bulls-Eye" and the other horse-fish swam away. "What about that barred window you were going to show me?"

They followed the wall of their private chamber along the side opposite the sea window. The artificial wall was a patchwork of masonry that filled in between pillars of natural stone. Back in a narrow alcove that reminded Bill of a streetcar vestibule, bars of light from the larger cavern world seeped in between bars of steel.

"You'll need these," said Windy, unfastening a pair of binoculars from his belt. "Get a focus on that peach-colored haze way to your right and you'll see the other city. I'll take myself back to the telephone."

FOR the next two hours Bill stayed at the window studying the lay of the land.

The binoculars brought him a miniature world—or was it two worlds? There were two kinds of creatures in it—very different creatures—and yet they had certain pronounced points of resemblance.

The spiny-men (including the spiny-women and spiny-children) lived among the uplands on the farther side of the river. That was the east side, if Bill's sense of direction served him. And what he chose to call uplands were, of course, actually beneath the level of the sea. But the main cavern was so vast and its ceiling so lofty that there was room for little hills and valleys, lakes, waterfalls, innumerable ramifying caves, and one river as broad as a boulevard.

This river appeared to divide the low arched mud huts of the horse-fish, on the west, from the statelier brick and mud homes of the spiny-men, on the east.

The river widened into a lake at what might be called its mouth. It couldn't be seen to flow into the sea, for at this depth nothing less than a system of artificial water gates could empty a river into the sea without allowing the sea to backwater into the whole cavern.

The cavern itself, Bill guessed, had been hollowed out by water during long ages past. Later some caprice of nature, perhaps an overflow of lava from some volcano up above, had spilled the gigantic icicles of rock across the mouth of the cavern. The skyscraper-sized icicles had melted together in a fortress against the sea. And somehow the creatures who had chosen to dwell here had managed to force out the impounded water.

But the horse-fish, at least, were still water-dwellers. Bill, turning the binoculars on the west bank of the river and its numerous inlets, observed that most of the gray mounds of the horse-fish city had no visible doors. The entrances were under water.

One matter was continually confusing, however. There were some houses that he could not classify. Worse, there were some creatures he could not classify. For farther up the stream, he noted, there ceased to be any clear-cut division between the city of the horse-fish and that of the spiny-men. The two appeared to be hopelessly merged. And from this distance he could not tell whether those little creatures molding pottery far up the river were horse-fish or spiny-men.

This was disturbing.

Bill's attention returned to the matter of sunlight. The hazy peach-colored light that had sifted through the ceiling far to the right, perhaps two miles distant, had turned to the amber of sunset, and now it melted into twilight gray.

So this undersea pocket had an outlet to the upper world, thought Bill. The city of the spiny-men had at least a limited daily taste of sunshine, blue sky, clouds.

AS THE last of daylight faded, the lines of artificial lights along the distant wall brought into view a zigzagging trail to the upper world.

A party of spiny-men was ascending that trail, carrying lanterns. Occasionally Bill thought he could see them waving their arms. Now and again he heard the rolling echoes of high voices that might have been laughter and shouting.

Then he caught sight of two figures descending the trail from the upper world, slowly moving down the incline toward the party with the lanterns. At once Bill guessed what was happening.

He chased back to the front of the chamber where Windy was still listening in at the silent phone.

"Let me have it, Windy!"

"Sure. Say—there's a lotta talk about a guy named *Vin-Vin*. Would that be your pal?"

"Sure as shootin'! Let me hear..."

"He's surprising 'em by dropping in unexpected. The phones are full of it."

Windy accepted the binoculars, trudged off to see what Bill had seen.

Bill adjusted the ebony posts to his head. In a moment the talk began to come in. It was confused, as if dozens of parties were talking—or rather *thinking*—to each other over the same connections.

But the outstanding news was the same throughout—*Vin-Vin* had returned for his "annual visit" much earlier than expected. There must be some reason. What could it be?

"Did Vin-Vin bring any converts with him?" many were asking.

"There's one guest," an answer came.

Occasionally, however, the messages would vary. There was one other exciting bit of gossip: The horse-fish had acquired some new prisoners.

"As soon as Vin-Vin is welcomed," some were saying, "he must be informed that the horse-fish have some upper-world prisoners."

The excitement was tremendous. The impact of these events obviously made big talk throughout the spiny-man community. And perhaps the horse-fish community as well. Bill picked up some startling implications.

For one thing, it was a strange fact that the horse-fish and the spiny-men employed a single interwoven system of communication. The horse-fish had access to the conversations of the spiny-men, and vice-versa.

Another striking fact was that George Vinson—if it was indeed Vinson—was evidently a big man in this underground world. The way his return was being heralded, Bill wondered if he might be the ruler.

At any rate these were Vinson's home people. That was a certainty—a very disturbing one. After all the years Bill had known Vin and been allowed to wonder over Vin's peculiarities—his inevitable gloves—his mane of fine hair that flowed over the back of his neck—at last Bill was seeing the man's roots for the first time.

IT MAY have been midnight or later when a silent phone message came to Bill.

He had almost dozed away, listening to the profuse speeches of welcome, hearing the flowery address by Thork, first assistant to the spiny-man ruler.

But soon after the whole underground world had seemingly tucked itself away for the night, a crystal-clear thought-wave came over the wires.

"Bill Pierce… I'm calling Bill Pierce… He may be here as a prisoner—oh, you're there, Bill. You made it! That's remarkable. I was horribly worried…"

"I'm all right, Vin," Bill spoke with enthusiasm. "Everything's okay, I guess."

"You sound nervous. Sick or anything?"

"No—that is, my backbone's healing up all right."

"Oh—too bad, fellow. So a horse-fish got you, eh? I was afraid of it. Those things can be deadly, you know. But if luck's with you, you come through *with a friend*. You know what I mean?"

"I guess so," said Bill. "Yellow Z—"

"I'll get in touch with you just as soon as I can. I'll be tied up with more or less ceremony through tomorrow. It's inescapable. You'll understand, Bill, after I've had a chance to explain."

Bill made no answer. He felt that his limping conversation was widening into a social chasm between them.

"Don't be downhearted, fellow." Vinson mustered in a hearty manner. "You know what I think?"

"What?"

"I think we'll find Bea Riley *alive*. I think the horse-fish took her by chance and got away with her. If they did they'll put her to work somewhere near these caverns. So don't lose hope...er..."

Vin broke off abruptly.

Bill struggled to suppress what leaped to the surface of his mind. Vinson, at the other end of the thought-wave telephone, must have sensed his confusion.

"You haven't seen her, have you, Bill... Oh, you *have*...alive?"

"Yes."

"You talked with her?"

"A little," Bill admitted.

"Hmmm..." Vin was slightly defensive. "Then she told you...about *me?*"

"She said she'd known you before. She mentioned you were a right guy—but she's always said that."

"We've got to save her, Bill. It's more than simply saving a life. She's a potential contributor to the race. My race. The future generations need her."

"I don't know anything about that," Bill retorted bluntly. "But *I* need her."

"I've got to see you, Bill. Where are you?"

BILL described the prison chamber. He mentioned that Windy Muff had found his way into the same jail.

"Have you seen anyone, other than horse-fish?" Vinson asked. "Any spiny-men, I mean?"

"Only one at close range," said Bill, and he described the fight that had taken place outside his window.

"That spiny-man was Thork, the king's lieutenant," said Vinson, and the mood of his thought-waves tightened with a self-enforced tolerance.

In a more eager humor he returned to the subject of Beatrice Riley.

"You don't happen to know," Vin's thoughts asked, "what they did with Bea—which way they took her—whether she was on foot or in a cylinder-cart—whether they put her to work on a batch of horse-fish eggs, or—"

"*Eggs!*"

Bill echoed the word with such amazement that Windy bounced up wondering what was the matter.

"If you're ordering breakfasts," Windy hissed, "make mine—"

Bill waved him away. But Windy's intrusion he knew was his own good fortune. It enabled him to suppress some answers that might otherwise have leaped over the phone from his mind to Vin's.

That mustn't happen. Bea Riley had made it plain that Bill's good friend Vin wasn't to cross her path.

"I'll talk with you later," Bill managed to say.

"I'll see you soon," Vin concluded as heartily as ever.

Bill, perspiring, moved away from the pink-globed phone, made for the fresh water spring. He needed a cool bath. That conversation had been an ordeal. For all he knew he might have revealed the very thoughts he meant to suppress.

CHAPTER NINE

A *slush-slush-slush* of a distant waterfall beat on Bill's ears. Other than this low intermittent roaring the night was silent. All lights had been dimmed throughout the cavern.

Slush-slush-slush—as rhythmic as the ticking of a grandfather clock.

From the barred window Bill could make out the narrow ribbon of water that plunged down a series of falls. The falls were beyond the spiny-men's city, in a high crevice-like branch of the cavern. Earlier in the evening, Bill knew, these falls hadn't been visible. They must have come with the high tides, he reasoned, they would go silent when the waters receded.

Slush-slush-slush. Bill went to work with a chunk of stone, synchronized his strokes to the rhythmic roar, chopped at the wall around the steel-barred window. Probably there were no guards to listen; at any rate the sounds of his battering would be submerged.

Windy roused up from sleep and took his turn at stone cutting while Bill rested.

"You're a bear for work," he said, as Bill went back to the task. Slowly the stubborn stone wore thin.

One steel bar had just begun to give when the lights of morning began to turn on.

Soon shafts of pink sunlight pressed through the vast ceiling over the eastern section of the big cavern. Meanwhile the wall grew brighter; voices of spiny-children began to echo from across the river. Nearer at hand the brilliant green heads of horse-fish nosed across ponds and inlets. Horse-fish padded across yards of wet sand, gathered in groups, gestured to each other in their own language of signs.

"See if there's anything on the phone, Windy," Bill ordered. "The day's beginning."

Windy groaned out of his sleep, yanked at his tousled red hair as if trying to remember where he was. Then he came up with a start.

"Didja get *through,* Bill?"

"Not quite."

"Dammit, I shouldn't have slept. Why'd you let me do it?"

"You were all in, Windy. Anyway one bar's beginning to loosen. But we'll have to slack up now..." Bill turn his head at a sudden noise. "Uh-oh, they're at the door."

Bill kicked some dust to hide the stone chips at his feet, brushed sand over his ripped and bleeding hands. By the time the circular steel door opened he was lying in the sand, pretending to be half-asleep.

The visitors were the four servant horse-fish bringing a tray of breakfast—more fried seafoods on plates of shell. The horse-fish looked around, satisfied themselves that all was well, and went on their way.

BILL and Windy breakfasted and listened at the telephone by turns, but no messages of consequence came through.

Meanwhile the horse-fish with the yellow Z on his sides paddled up to the sea-window to begin his day of watching.

"He makes me nervous," Windy muttered, casting sidewise glances at the sea cavern.

"I wish I could get him on the phone once and see what's eating on him," said Bill. "He's going to cramp our style. Especially if he figures out what we're up to."

"He can't see our escape window from his post," said Windy. "We could go ahead—"

"Risky," said Bill. "The tide's going down and the waterfall has nearly stopped. We'd be heard. But we may have to take a chance—"

Bill broke off with a low whistle. He brushed his breakfast aside and sprang to the sea window. *A cylinder was floating past.*

"That's your gal friend again, ain't it?" said Windy.

Bill scarcely heard, he was too busy pounding on the window and beckoning. The upper third of the upright cylinder was floating above the surface of the water. Through the transparent domed lid he could see Beatrice. The same instrument was clamped to her head. Her eyes were closed. She looked pale. She was sleeping. Or was she ill—or even—

Sharp chills pierced through Bill's arms down to his fingertips.

But no, she wasn't dead. She was breathing slowly. He could see her plainly. The cylinder was wafted along by sluggish currents. Passing within twenty feet of the big window it caught light from the prison chamber.

Bill watched, motionless, half hypnotized by the sight. Bea's pallid face revealed such a resigned calmness and patience. As ever, there was that deep, mysterious beauty—

Bill caught his breath.

The cylinder was floating past, now, turning so he could no longer see her.

A strange terror seized him. He drew back from the window clenching his fists. His dread of the unknown suddenly welled up into a nameless horror.

"I don't know what's happening. Watch her, Windy, till I—"

His feet were ahead of his words. He dashed back to the other end of the chamber and into the little stonewalled vestibule with the barred window. He rattled the loosened bar.

Then he heard Windy calling him to come back.

"Look, Bill. What's Yellow Z up to?"

Bill returned on the run. In the preceding moments he had ignored the curious blinking eyes of the horse-fish, but now he saw what the creature was doing. Yellow Z was pushing the cylinder back toward the window, turning it so that the girl's face was toward them.

"How'd *he* know I wanted her to come back?" Bill uttered nervously.

"Damned if he ain't on our side!" Windy chuckled.

"Either that or he's scheming. What the hell…"

THE yellow-marked horse-fish whirled the cylinder with astonishing suddenness, grabbed it by a choice hand-hold and went swimming off with it as hard as he could go.

Bill smacked his head against the glass in his eagerness to see where the cylinder was going. That end of the underground lake was too dark to see far. Bill watched until the object diminished to shadowy bubble. It cut an arc through the dark waters and disappeared from sight. Bill stepped down from the window.

"That damn horse-fish," Windy muttered, "has got a screw loose. He's the most inconsistent critter—"

"I've gotta get out of here!" Bill yelled, kicking at the sand.

"Didn't he fight you one minute and save you the next…?" Windy's eyes then widened. "*Look, Bill!* There's some more spiny-men and horse-fish comin'. Yellow Z musta seen 'em. That's probably why he took off so fast."

Bill whirled back to the window in time to see a black-haired spiny-man swim into view. It was the same stony-featured spiny-man who had fought the day before. Thork was the name, Bill recalled. This fellow, according to the mental telephone messages, was the lieutenant to the king.

The swimmer stopped directly before the window, turned to beckon to someone back of him. Over the silver-tinted waters to the east a few other swimming creatures were following in his wake.

Thork waited, watching them approach. He momentarily turned his head toward the prison window, and his brief stare at Bill and Windy brought a sour scowl to his face. He did not appear to be particularly surprised—and Bill guessed that he had probably heard rumors of their capture. He shrugged and looked away.

Now the rest of the party swam into view—three horse-fish and one more spiny-man. It was not a chase this time. It was more nearly a council. Thork had evidently led the others to this spot to explain what had happened in the previous day's altercation, for he began talking and pointing with great animation. A faint rumble of his low voice echoed through the glass, though Bill could understand nothing.

But obviously the three horse-fish were listening closely. They punctuated Thork's rapid-fire story with gestures, apparently causing him to change his claims.

Then, for the first time, the face of the second spiny-man came into view. It might have struck Bill as being a handsome face for a human creature whose backbone was lined with little horn-like spines, and whose fingers were connected with webs. But this face was more than handsome—it was intelligent, honest—and definitely familiar.

It was George Vinson.

Bill should have been prepared for the shock. But somehow he was not. He had never seen Vin before except as a neat little man dressed in white, and never without white gloves. Never without his artistic head of hair flowing loosely to the back of his neck.

In the heat of the conference with Thork and the three horse-fish, George Vinson's bright beady eyes shot a look at Bill. It was a look that said, "I know you're there; friend. I'll get to you when this job's over. One trouble at a time. I'm a busy man down in this world."

IT was startling how much genuine importance there was about Vinson, even when stripped of his fine clothes and swimming about in bathing trunks. Even when arguing with a fellow spiny-man and three horse-fish. When Vin spoke, his words counted.

And they were counting now. He was wasting no words. The horse-fish nodded their agreement. Thork appeared to be swallowing a bitter pill, but he finally nodded too.

Vin gave a wave that seemed to indicate everything was settled.

Then Thork did some more pointing, this time in the direction that Yellow Z had swum away with the cylinder.

"Thork's changed the subject," Windy observed shrewdly. "He lost his argument about the fight, so he's tryin' to start somethin' else."

Bill breathed uneasily. "Do you suppose he saw Bea?"

"What if he did?" said Windy. "Would that be bad?"

"Plenty. She doesn't want to be seen by these spiny-men. She's got some mysterious connections down here. She'll be very upset if they find her. Who knows, rather than face them, she might—" Bill's pent-up agitation then broke loose in a violent snarl. *"I've got to get out of this trap!"*

He caught himself, though, and stopped his nervous pacing. The whole group outside the window was watching him. Expressions of curiosity were on their faces.

"They're talkin' about her, all right, and us too," Windy whispered. "They'll be in here quizzin' us next. If they do, I won't know whether I'm comin' or goin.' And that's the devil's truth... There they go."

Bill saw Vin disperse the party with a wave of his webbed hand. But the creatures did not all swim away in the same direction. The stony-faced Thork, shooting another cold glance into the prison chamber, sped off in the direction Yellow Z had taken the cylinder.

The instant the sea-window was cleared of spiny-men and horse-fish, Bill strode back to the other corner of the chamber. He grabbed a rock and went to work battering the steel bar again.

Windy spelled him off. In a matter of minutes they succeeded in jerking the first bar out of its sockets. But Bill jammed it back and he and Windy both ducked—none too soon. A gang of horse-fish led by "Bull's-Eye" had come into view. Bill could hear them padding along the sandy trail.

Presently they were out of hearing. But other footsteps were approaching. A knock sounded at the circular metal door.

"It's Vin, Bill," came the voice from the other side of the door. "I had to come back the long way around. Are you all right in there? Plenty of food and water?"

"We're okay," said Bill.

"Then I'll settle up this murder mess of Thork's before I come back to get you out," Vin called. "These horse-fish have their rights, you know, and it pays to handle them with gloves. You won't worry if it's two or three hours?"

"We won't worry," said Bill.

THERE was a moment of silence. Bill realized his answers had been terse, far from cordial. He added, "Take your time, Vin."

"That's the spirit, Bill." Vin's heartiness was quick to respond. "I'll have this door open before noon. And you must be ready to tell me what you know about Bea."

Another silence.

"Did you hear what I said, Bill? You'll have to help me with Bea."

"I heard."

"Good. We'll have to work some tall strategy on the horse-fish to get her. They're killers, you know, under certain conditions. It's a constant job to hold down the number of fights with them. And we're having to bargain with them, just now, for too many favors. Do you understand the source of their treachery, Bill?"

"Not altogether." Bill was kneeling at the keyhole of the circular door, listening eagerly.

"Then I'd better tip you off right now," came Vinson's voice. "They can be your best friends—or your worst enemies. They're our cousins, in a sense, and they've got a streak of intelligence you won't find a match for anywhere in the upper world. But their emotions are unstable. Do you understand?"

"Yes," said Bill.

"Their prickly spines may not look like blotters, but that's exactly what they are. Blotters. They absorb the emotions and desires and sentiments of other creatures. If one of them tears along your backbone while he's fighting you, he picks up a whole set of feelings *from you.*"

"So that's it!" Bill gasped. "That's why Yellow Z let me off easy after that first gash."

"Right. *Your* feelings became *his* feelings. That's why they're treacherous, Bill. You may think you've got a horse-fish *friend*—one that'll stall off all possible trouble—but if he scrapes the back of *your enemy* and picks up a new set of feelings—*look out.*"

"I get it," said Bill.

"Now you see what we've got to work with," Vinson concluded. "The sooner we can get Beatrice out of their clutches, without upsetting the apple cart, the better for everyone. And believe me, Bill, the city of spiny-men will have one tall celebration when they learn that Bea—Bea has come back to them. So long, Bill."

"Wait. Are you still there?" Bill called at the keyhole.

"Yes?"

"What was this business you mentioned over the thought-phone? Something about eggs?"

"Oh, that. I'll tell you when I come back."

Bill and Windy listened until the footsteps retreated out of hearing. Then they slipped back to the window.

"Any last minute instructions, Bill?" Windy asked.

"Keep your ears to the phone, Windy. If the horse-fish miss me tell 'em I buried myself under the sand for a nap. Or tell 'em nothing."

With that Bill hoisted himself to the window and wormed through. He turned back to Windy for a last word.

"If you don't hear from me within twenty-four hours, you'll know Bea and I have sneaked through to the surface. Then you can tell Vin thanks, but we couldn't use his help."

CHAPTER TEN

BILL moved with the stealth of a leopard. He picked his course from shadow to shadow.

He knew the cavern lake could be reached only by a roundabout trail. There was hardly a chance he could reach Bea ahead of Thork. He'd hung back like a docile prisoner too long.

But his blood was boiling now. He cursed himself with every leap and bound for letting Bea stay in the cylinder. Now she'd be grabbed by the spiny-men—the very thing she feared most.

Why did she abhor them so?

Bill wasn't sure. But he had a dozen vague guesses—all of them too horrible to face. He was blind to everything, now, except getting her out of this weird hole.

Every time Bill dashed past a pink-lighted pole he felt like stopping to see what new talk was flying through the cave. Thork had probably found her—perhaps the whole spiny-man city knew by now.

And would that city prepare a welcome for her, as Vin had predicted? *What was the spiny-men's city to Bea?* The hot blood of an almost insane anguish pounded through Bill's arteries.

Bea must belong here!

But how could she? Her body was the perfect body of a human being. In the thousands of public appearances she had made in her abbreviated diving costume, her splendid physique had never failed to charm the audience. In the graceful lines of her back there wasn't a hint of spiny-men features. Nor were there any signs of webs between her fingers or toes.

She couldn't be a spiny-woman! And yet—

Bill couldn't throw the thought out of his mind. Pictures flooded upon him—the views he had caught while studying the spiny-men's city through the binoculars.

Yes, he had seen all varieties of spiny-folk. Some had merged indistinguishably with the horse-fish. On the other hand some had looked so much like upper-world men, from his distance, that it had left him wondering about it.

Now Bill was nearly a mile east of his prison cavern. The river's waters, piled deep against the artificial doorways to the sea, were not far ahead. He had followed the trails along the base of the south wall to keep his distance from scattered groups of horse-fish going about their work.

Bill stopped, slipped into a rocky crevice. A party of horse-fish was approaching. He crowded against the rock.

THE ten or twelve female horse-fish passed without seeing him. They had evidently just returned from the open sea, for they were lugging armloads of fresh seaweed. Bill must be on the right trail.

He raced on. Wherever scraps of seaweed had dropped he grabbed them up on the run and slapped them over his shoulders for camouflage.

At last, taking a chance on being seen from the houses on either side of the river, he slipped up a steep pathway to an opening in the vast curtain of lava rock. Dripping seaweeds had been dragged through the narrow A-shaped pass. Ahead was darkness.

Then his eyes adjusted, he saw the silver-edged waters at his feet. This had to be the cavern lake.

Shaking off the cloak of seaweeds, he plunged in and swam back to the west. He knew the speed he could hold for distance swimming. The unlighted cavern might have been an entrance to the end of the world. The black waters were devoid of dimensions, to Bill's eyes. Only the dim outlines of mammoth stone icicles, wet from seepage, gave the cavern any form whatsoever.

Then Bill began to pass big, lighted windows. Here again were those ubiquitous signs of the mechanical civilization of upper-world men.

Here was a series of pumping stations. Both spiny-men and horse-fish were working the big crude waterpower machines.

Farther on Bill swam past the pink-lighted windows of prison chambers. The rock-walled rooms, though they contained glowing telephones, were empty, for their circular doors stood open. Near the sea-window of one cell an old dry human skull grinned out at Bill—or was it a spiny-man skull?

In either case, it testified to a tragedy of years ago, perhaps starvation, or a battle to death, or an insane suicide.

Now Bill swam past the cell he recognized. He caught a brief sight of Windy Muff with his head at the telephone, his eyes blinking up at the walls. Windy was a statue of bewilderment. Whether the thought-phone was alive with strange messages or whether Windy was day dreaming of the stories he would tell if he ever got back, Bill could only wonder.

Without slackening his strokes Bill sped on.

Then something was swimming toward him. He surface-dived. He put many yards back of him before he crawled back to the surface.

The swimming form was back of him now, following in his wake.

Four times he surface-dived, to cut along under the waters at high speed. Then a streak of light cut the race short. The swimming form was Yellow Z.

Still a friend? With an odd sensation of self-consciousness Bill spoke aloud.

"If you're on my side, fellow, take me to that floating cylinder."

He hung back as the horse-fish cut ahead of him.

YELLOW Z swam in a wide arc to the right, Bill in his wake. The cavern lake was narrowing. Slits of light through the ceiling hundreds of feet overhead restored Bill's sense of direction. But those narrow vertical gashes offered no hope of escape.

Suddenly Yellow Z grabbed Bill by the hand and jerked him into the shadowed waters. Yellow Z crawled up on a ledge of dry rock and peeked over cautiously. Bill followed his example.

Sounds of splashing and paddling echoed through the lake-filled canyon. At the bend the rush of swimming figures came into view.

"Thork, again!" Bill muttered under his breath. "And Bull's-Eye."

But the two creatures weren't alone. A gang of horse-fish was on their trail. Thork had got himself into another mess with the horse-fish...

This time Bill saw that Thork was avoiding a fight. Or more accurately, Bull's-Eye was preventing it. The white-dotted horse-fish was darting back and forth, keeping the rest of the pursuing horse-fish at bay while Thork swam full speed ahead.

His course was back toward the cities—over the same waters Bill had just come. And now Bill saw, with immense relief, that the glass-domed cylinder was in full view almost directly below him.

It was still floating upright, still lighted, still occupied.

Bea's uptilted face was chalk-white and her eyes were closed. She was half-reclining, and the slow rhythmic rise and fall of her breasts told that she was sleeping easily. The instruments at her head had not been moved since he last saw her being towed away from the prison window.

This, then, was where Yellow Z had brought her for safe hiding. And here the lieutenant of the spiny-men had followed.

But Thork's visit had just now been foiled by the savage horse-fish. The splashing echoes of that chase were fading. This moment was Bill's chance.

"Here goes, Yellow Z!" he said aloud. "We're going to crack this safe before you can wink your little red eyes."

The hand of Yellow Z slapped over Bill's wrist as Bill was lowering himself over the ledge. But Bill was in no mood to be restrained. He jerked free, slipped into the water, swam once around the cylinder, and began jerking all the valve levers furiously.

He paid no attention when Yellow Z caught him by the shoulder. He shook the webbed hand off, for now the valves were opening and he found a way in.

He caught half a breath, dived into the water-filled aperture at the cylinder's base. Once he had to kick off Yellow Z's troublesome grab at his ankle. Then he was free to rise through the valves toward the upper floor.

"Bea! Bea!" he called, as he climbed upward. "You've got to get out of here, Bea. Wake up! The spiny-men know you're here. They're laying for you!"

AS HE came up to the level where Bea's feet rested he was aware that something more than water had drenched his body during his ascent through the series of floors. A syrupy liquid spilled over his shoulders, and with it came a hundred tickling and scratching sensations. As if he'd broken through a wall of eggs.

The light from the dome of the cylinder blazed down on his dripping body and he saw.

The mess *was* broken eggs—dozens of them. Their brittle white shells had crushed at his touch and spilled their contents.

Bill couldn't be bothered. He gave his gooey hands a swipe against the cylinder walls, all the while shouting at Beatrice. He slapped her feet. Then rising to stand beside her, he jerked the instruments off her head.

Her eyelids lifted heavily, then fell closed.

"It's me!" Bill uttered. "You've got to wake up, Bea!"

He slapped her cheeks briskly. Her head dropped forward, her eyes were trying to open. Still, her arms hung so limply that Bill knew this was more than the stupor of sleep. It was exhaustion.

"Bill," she whispered faintly. "It's you?"

"Bea, you know it is. Come on. Snap out of it."

He tried to take her up in his arms. It was difficult to help her when her body was so limp.

"Where are we, Bill?"

"Getting out of here." Bill puffed as he dragged her down through the mess of broken shells, down into the water-filled valves. "Hold your breath, Bea. Here we go."

Then they were out in the cool waters. Bea was swimming listlessly on her back.

"Hurry, honey," Bill kept urging.

"I'm trying," she said. "But I'm so weak—hungry—"

"Poor kid—you might have died in that cylinder."

"Cylinder... Oh!" she gasped.

In the diminishing light Bill saw her eyes widen. She changed to a breaststroke, quickening her speed.

He glanced back. Yellow Z hadn't followed. Instead the friendly horse-fish had again mounted the ledge, and there he sat as motionless as a moody gargoyle on a cathedral wall.

FOR THE next twenty minutes Bea swam hard, and Bill knew she had no energy for talking.

But when they approached the pink lights of the prison windows, she slackened her pace.

"We'd better cut around," she said. "If the natives find out I've come back—"

"They already know, Bea," said Bill. "That's why—"

"*Who* knows?"

"Thork, the king's lieutenant. He followed to the cylinder, but the horse-fish drove him off."

"Oh!"

Her faint tone conveyed a secret hurt that was too deep for words. Then as if bristling spines were suddenly plunged into her flesh she cried.

"Bill! *How* did you get me out?"

"Through the valves."

"I mean, *how—without breaking the eggs?*" Her voice was wild with terror. "You didn't—"

"I busted 'em all over myself," said Bill. "I didn't know they were in there. Why?"

"Oh, Bill!" she was sobbing bitterly. She caught a muffled breath, let her face drop under the surface, and swam on so fast that Bill was left more than a length behind.

CHAPTER ELEVEN

WHEN they reached the A-shaped pass to the main cavern Bea dropped on the bank utterly exhausted. Bill lifted her up into his arms and carried her.

But the webs of light along the vast cavern wall opened her languorous eyes.

"Bill," she breathed. "We've got to hide—quick."

"Just from the spiny-men—or the horse-fish too?"

"Oh, you poor idiot!" she cried angrily. "The maddest spiny-man would never hope to live twenty-four hours if he had crushed a horse-fish's eggs. It's fatal."

Bill felt the weight of tragedy hovering, about to descend. Every minute of his return swim he'd suspected this was coming, and yet he'd kidded himself with the silly hope it wouldn't be so serious.

"Then they'll *all* be sent out to capture me—"

"Bill, frankly it would have been a lot easier if you'd just taken poison—and then given a dose to me."

"To *you!*" Bill cried. "You didn't commit the blunder. I was the one. If they think they can catch me and kill me for it, let them try. But I'll clear you of any wrongdoing if it's the last thing I—"

"Bill, you can't. I'm the *guiltiest,* in their eyes," she whispered hoarsely. "I was charged with *giving my thoughts* to those embryo horse-fish. I pledged I'd do it. That was my job…"

"You're not serious…"

"Don't look at me so, Bill. You can't appreciate it," Bea moaned, "until you've lived down here. But there's a streak of something different in these green sea creatures—an uncanny streak of wisdom that's not matched anywhere in nature. Not even the smartest upper-world people can store up knowledge the way these horse-fish can."

"What *are* you talking about? Is this some ungodly superstition?"

"It's a quirk of nature, Bill. They more or less *inherit* men's thoughts. They're like sponges or blotters. Even before they hatch out of eggs, they begin to take on their patterns of thought. It's very strange to you, I suppose—"

"It's remarkable—but what kind of thoughts could you possibly transfer to unhatched eggs, cooped up in that cylinder?"

"Any and all thoughts that pass through my mind. I just lay there daydreaming and sleeping. Whether I happen to dream about diving exhibitions or sailing back to the States or reading books, there were sure to be plenty of elementary ideas mixed in."

"Such as?"

"Well, elementary functions like walking and talking, the ability to read, getting along peaceably with other creatures, feelings of loyalty to your own friends—there are hundreds of such things involved in any situations you happen to think about. When *upper-world* babies are born they don't know anything about these things. They don't even know how to speak a language. But these baby horse-fish actually come into the world with a fair knowledge of English or other languages."

BILL frowned darkly. He felt a twinge of something akin to jealousy. After what he'd seen he couldn't doubt these weird facts, but he didn't welcome them. To think that these silent little water beasts could soak up men's thought waves with no effort—at no cost—*for no good,* was truly frightening.

"Why haven't the spiny-men eradicated them?" he asked. "It's hard for me to see a thing good about them. They seem to be more treacherous than poison snakes—"

"And friendlier than any human beings, and more helpful—*after* they've absorbed the right thought-waves," said Bea. "These thought-wave phones throughout the caverns help keep them friendly. And still, they and the spiny-men are forever clashing…"

Her eyelids closed. Her voice trailed away.

"You've got to have some food and rest before we can chance a dash out of this place," Bill whispered. "We've got to pick the right moment—"

"As if it mattered," she nearly whispered. "We'll never get past them."

He carried her along a perilous shelf of rock high above the river. There were no foot tracks up here. The beams from the nearest wall lights rarely reached up to this level.

"I used to climb this trail when I was a little girl," Bea said. "I would come up here and spy on both cities. I saw so much trouble between the two sides of the river that I grew to hate it all."

"We'll soon be out of here—for good," said Bill. "Here's a shadowed spot. You've got to lie dawn and rest before we go on."

"Bill, we'll never make it," she sobbed quietly, lying down on the warm rock and folding her arm under her head for a pillow. "There's not a chance in a thousand that the horse-fish will let us live, after what's happened. You see, that's why they took me off the boat in the first place—to care for those eggs."

Bill sat down near her, folded his arms.

"Did they know it was you—a native?" he asked.

"Not at first. They'd simply swam out to capture an upper-world female."

"Then they go in for kidnapping as a regular sport?" Bill muttered.

"They only steal a new upper-world person when they have a need. Usually their captive mothers don't live many years. Sometimes only a few months."

"Bea! You knew this...and yet you submitted—"

"They recognized me as soon as I got down here," she looked up at Bill guiltily. "They remembered me as a spiny-girl from across the river. You knew, of course, that I *am*—"

"I only guessed," said Bill quietly, avoiding her eyes. "But not until after Windy and I were captured."

"They recognized me," she went on, "as a native who had been away for a few years. So I confided in them—and made a bargain."

"Yes?"

"I admitted I was a runaway. I couldn't endure living down here. But if they would promise me my freedom afterward, and *yours,* I would go ahead and be the 'thought-mother' to this one batch of eggs. In a few days it would have been over."

Bill understood. At first he was not clear as to why the horse-fish had followed their theft of Bea with a similar kidnapping of Windy Muff. But Beatrice explained that that, too, was customary. The horse-fish always tried to furnish their captured females with mates. In this case, Bill understood, they had failed to pull Maribeau the scientist overboard, but had succeeded in getting Windy Muff.

Bill shuddered as he turned these bizarre customs over in his mind. But practical considerations shook him into action.

"I know where I can get some food," he said, "without being seen. And if there's a chance to listen in at a phone—"

"Just food," said Beatrice. "You won't want to hear what they're saying by now."

CHAPTER TWELVE

BILL backtracked over his old trail to the barred window of his prison cell. He called in a whisper. Windy Muff's voice answered him.

"Darned if I didn't think you were hissin' over the phone," said Windy. "Why don't you come around to the door and walk in? It's wide open."

"How come?"

"Vinson's been here and gone. He came to turn us loose and give us a free tour of the city. But he found you gone, and I told him I wouldn't budge from this spot till you came back."

While Bill entered by the door and gathered up the food Windy had saved for him, the latter poured forth the exciting news as fast as he could jabber.

Vin's eyes had blazed cold fire, Windy said, to learn that Bill had broken out and gone to find Bea. Vin had said it was a deadly thing to do, and bad judgment.

"So you told him everything?" asked Bill.

"Yep. I've always said my reputation for bein' a liar wasn't deserved. Well, he went on his way, sayin' we should both report to him as soon as possible."

"Go and report to him," said Bill sharply. "But tell him not to look for me."

Bill started off, but Windy blocked his path at the door. "Vin was right, was he? You ran into trouble?"

"Plenty of it," Bill admitted. In a few words he related what had happened at the west end of the sea cavern. He concluded by stating his doubts whether Yellow Z was still a friend, after what he'd done. "Anyway, they'll be after me—

and Bea too—and she's got to pick up a bit of strength before we can make a break for the top. So long, Windy."

"Good luck, Bill…"

Back along the shadowed wall trail Bill sprinted. By now the protective shadows were familiar. In a few moments he was crawling the high narrow ridge that arched above the river out of reach of the lights.

Bea was not sleeping as he had hoped. She had crawled several yards beyond the sheltered spot where he had left her. She was crowding close to the overhanging edge, listening.

Her eyes flicked at Bill as he approached, inviting him to come join her. She was listening to the clattering voices rising from the excited spiny-man city. The use of some kind of strange microphonic equipment, along with the unusual acoustics of the cavern world, made their voices somewhat audible.

"The tension is tight already, Bill," she whispered. "They're stirred up on both sides of the river. And have you seen the ascent?"

SHE pointed to the zigzag trail to the upper-world. Bill could see groups of spiny-men stationed near the top. Still further up was a cluster of horse-fish.

"We're not going to get out, Bill. They'll see to that."

"By this time they all know what happened to the eggs, I suppose?"

"Yes. Yellow Z and some others dragged the cylinder back into the horse-fish city only a few minutes ago."

"How'd the horse-fish take it?"

"It's a good thing they can't cry out loud," said Bea. "Look. Those columns swimming in figures and circles at the west side of the river are expressing their anguish and grief."

"Some are crossing the river," Bill observed.

"And there have been minor fights with spiny-men. It's times like these that bring up all the old animosities. All my life down here I've watched it. These two cities live forever on the verge of war."

Bea ate and slept while Bill kept vigil.

Toward night a great mass meeting came together on the east bank of the river. It was formally opened by the ruler of the spiny-men himself. Bea gasped to see the aged, sharp-backed old creature totter down the path from the triple-domed mud palace.

"That's a rare sight," Bea said. "They don't see him except on the most important occasions."

"What are they going to do?"

"I don't know. I never saw the horse-fish and spiny-men mass together before."

"Do the horse-fish have a king too?"

Bea shook her head. That was one great reason for the constant trouble with the green sea-creatures. They weren't emotionally stable. One of their number might be in favor as a leader for a time—but if he chanced to stab his spine into the back of a spiny-man—or a native islander of the upper-world—he'd absorb a new temperament.

"You can't have rulers or followers among folks that are always changing their natures," Bea said. "So there's just the one king—that old white-haired spiny-man."

Bill listened. In a quaking voice that spoke the tongue of an aged English sea captain the spiny-man king called the mass meeting to order. The hundreds of horse-fish, ranged along the river's edge, were listening attentively. Closer around the mud dais were the clusters of spiny-men, women, and children.

The king, thought Bill, was little more than a figurehead. He recited a remarkable legend from memory—a fanciful tale of the shipwreck of centuries ago, and the ravages of a volcano and a tidal wave that left a band of English explorers imprisoned here.

THEN his archaic singsong recitation hinted that there was an amazing fusion of two kinds of animal life—man and horse-fish—the strange nature of which only the gods might explain. But the ancient English explorers need not be ashamed of that amazing fusion, for nothing less could have won the victory of survival.

This brought the king's recitation down to the present century when the new and wonderful race of spiny-men had emerged. It was the triumphant blend of the best qualities of men and horse-fish.

And at last, so the king's story went, trade and commerce had been established with the upper-world, so that sealocks and pumps and electrical miracles had been procured.

Then, with a stereotyped promise that the spiny-men were destined to become the great earth-dwelling race of the future, the king bowed low, turned, and tottered back to his tripled-domed mud palace at the foot of the ascent.

Now Thork, the hard-bitten lieutenant, took charge. The real business of the day began.

"No one denies that the horse-fish have their rights," he began, and with his opening words the spines of the horse-fish began to bristle. "But many is the time that we spiny-men have been too liberal with the rights of the horse-fish." Thork paused momentarily. "You are asking me for examples? Don't be absurd…"

Bill saw what was going on. Many of the horse-fish were wearing portable telephones and were shooting questions to Thork, no doubt. For the phones made their thoughts transport to Thork's mind, who was likewise wearing a phone unit on his head. As fast as he spoke he was picking up their mental reactions. He came back at them angrily.

"On the other rare occasions when an upper-world innocent has blundered into our world and been placed in one of your sacred cylinders, and inadvertently destroys some of the eggs during hatching season, what do you do? You kill him. And we spiny-men don't raise a hand, because we've gotten into the habit of pampering you and your rights..."

Bill whispered, "Is that bird getting ready to take our sides?"

Bea doubted it. "I never knew him to champion any outsider," she said, never taking her eyes off the crowd below her.

Thork's challenge continued. "But this time you've dragged a spiny-girl into your egg-training ritual. And you've had a disaster. Well, let me warn you. *This* side of the river is waiting to welcome that girl. We've been waiting a long time for her to come back."

Some of the horse-fish were removing their headphones by this time, and that, Bill knew, meant they didn't want their thoughts to be conveyed.

"In fact," Thork went on, "this spiny-girl is someone *I've* been particularly waiting for, ever since we let her go away to be educated... And if she's within earshot of my voice, I want her to know that *she's* not going to pay for the broken eggs. She's our own. There'll be war in camp if you make one move to harm her..."

Suddenly the whole riverbank of green seemed to fold in slowly toward the spiny-men. Not with a rush. Just a slow turtle-paced movement. The green bags some were carrying, Bea whispered, contained deadly scorpion fish, their favorite weapons.

"Stand where you are, horse-fish!" The full-voiced command rang from the throat of George Vinson, who had suddenly sprung to the dais. "Thork isn't the only voice in this city. Listen to *me...*"

The wave of slowly advancing horse-fish stopped. The ranks of the spiny-men, bristling for trouble, suddenly quieted. It was plain that the black-haired little mediator was respected by both sides of the underground world. At once he launched a feverish plea for peace and harmony.

The girl was also *his* friend, he said; and so was the man who had broken jail and gone to find her. But there were stouter reasons than these for keeping peace. There was the vision of great destiny that the spiny-men held.

"And this vision, as I have told you so many times," George Vinson pleaded, *"must* have the cooperation of the most highly developed upper-world men *and* the most highly developed horse-fish. The biological contributions of both are indispensable."

Bill gasped, "Biological!" He looked to Bea for an answer.

"That's George Vinson's big idea," she whispered. She drew closer to Bill and answered his questions.

Yes, she had expected to marry an upper-world man. A mixing of spiny-folk with upper-world folk, she had been taught, was the only way this superior underground race would breed out the damning marks which their crossing with horse-fish had left on them—webbed hands and feet, and a row of more or less conspicuous spines over the backbone. So, as a child, Bea had been destined to marry an upper-worlder.

And there were many such upper-world guests—perhaps two or three a year. It was George Vinson's difficult task to go to the upper-world and spread the gospel of a finer race and to bring converts back with him. The finest corals and pearls from the nearby seas were spent to make him a wealthy and respected missionary. Many of his converts now lived here; others died through misfortunate dealings with the horse-fish; some had even fled.

"You say you *were* to have married an upper-world man?" Bill asked.

"They decreed otherwise as soon as they saw I was becoming a young woman—*without* spines or webs. Then they decided I should go to the upper-world for an education," Bea sighed, "because I would not be conspicuous. When I came back a suitable match would be made for me here."

Bill scowled. "When had you intended coming back?"

"Never," said Bea. "I loved the upper-world. I hated all this—even Vin with his fine theories. That's why I've almost hated myself. Because at heart I know I'm a traitor."

BILL slipped his arm around her, patting her shoulder gently. She was trembling. "I'm going to see that you marry an upper-world man as soon as I can get you out of here." Bill looked down into her clear eyes. He whispered hoarsely, "I don't know about these spiny-men theories. And all this vision business that Vin used to try to pound into my head—it's way over my head. But I've got my own vision, Bea. It begins right here, with me telling you I love you—and you telling me the same… Say it, won't you, Bea?"

"You make it sound so easy, Bill," she whispered. Her face lifted slightly toward his. He crushed her lips in the warmth of his kisses.

The speeches continued to well up from somewhere below the ledge, but Bill ceased to hear them. The ocean's high tide began to spill down through the cavern in rhythmic gushes. But Bill was oblivious to roaring waterfalls. He heard nothing but the pounding of Bea's heart, and his own, and the enchanting whispers from the lips he loved to kiss.

"You've got to promise you'll marry me, Bea. If you will, all the spiny-men and horse-fish together won't be able to keep us down here… Say it, won't you?"

"I do love you, Bill," she said softly. "I can't deny it... But I'll never marry you. Don't look so crushed, Bill. Can't you see, it wouldn't be fair to you—or to our children, because—because I'm a spiny-woman—and you—you belong to the wonderful world up there..."

CHAPTER THIRTEEN

VIBRANT words were still ringing from the river's bank below them. Dazed and shattered, his attention returned to the weird meeting.

"Have you a chance to become the masters of the world?"

Bill was surprised to see the scientist, Jean Maribeau, wrapping the heterogeneous audience into a magic spell. George Vinson had called upon him, as an authority from the outside world, to express the opinions he had formed in his recent hours of observation.

"That's Vin's supreme strategy for keeping peace," Bea said in a low voice, straining at the cliff's edge to catch every word.

Bill was surprised to see how her interest had quickened. The words of an upper-world scientist might strike a new responsive chord—

"As a *scientist* I say that no creatures ever lived who have a better chance *to inherit the earth* than you spiny-men... I do not overlook the contributions from both of your lines of ancestors. This instantaneous absorption of knowledge—an ability that is being bred into your race through your kinship with the horse-fish—is destined to make the Earth's new man superior to the old."

Many horse-fish were nodding their agreement, holding their heads proudly.

"In addition," Maribeau went on, "it goes without saying that the vast stores of knowledge from the upper-world men will become your birthright... But I must be brutally frank. There are not enough of you—spiny-men and horse-fish combined—to so much as conquer the island village over your heads.

"What does this mean? It means that *you, the spiny-men, cannot afford to lose one potential father or mother.* If Vin-Vin is able to convert upper-world men to this cause, their biological contributions will bend the race toward the ultimate triumph. But let me be frank again, at the risk of being brutal. You creatures, you horse-fish—"

THE scientist hesitated, as if catching warnings from the ranks of the speechless green creatures.

"The race of horse-fish must not seek to increase their numbers. Your contributions to the spiny-men have been made. Your flashy intellect has taken root among them. They now have the handicaps of partial spines and webs. *But they must not have the handicap of speechlessness. That would be fatal to their progress.* So—"

Horse-fish began to hoist their heads belligerently.

"So—you sea creatures who have no tongues—and that goes for every purebred horse-fish I've observed—you must cease to reproduce. I advise you all to destroy your own eggs, and to commit, what some might call, racial suicide…"

The horse-fish rose up on their hind legs. Dozens of them waved their arms. Some reached into their green bags and seized their deadly scorpion fish. Still, something held them back. To Bill it seemed that a single battle cry would have galvanized them into an army plunging forward to attack. But without that battle cry they were only so many separate clusters of individuals.

Yet their bluff forced the speaker to a quick conclusion. He ended by reminding them of the immortality that awaited all of them if they could inherit the earth. Evolution, he said, was *sympodial.* It left many races out on a dead limb. But now it could become a conscious process, an instrument in their own hands. And the present upper-world race of men would pass out of existence because it had become over-specialized.

"Don't forget that human life came forth from the sea," Maribeau nearly shouted, raising his arms dramatically. "If a new race of man evolves, he must receive his fresh impetus from that cradle of all life—the sea."

These words were almost more than Bill could digest. It was hard to believe that the horse-fish could allow their emotions to go up and down like a thermometer. One moment they were enraged to be told they should commit racial suicide. The next they were inflated by thoughts of their wonderful contributions to their descendants.

Once more they had stopped in their tracks, the whole body of nervous horse-fish, listening, considering.

"He's got them coming his way again," Bill whispered to Bea. "It puts them and the spiny-men back on an even keel."

Bea, her eyes intent upon the scene below, made a surprising answer. "I can take it. For the first time I'm getting a glimmer of the big, wonderful thing Vin's been preaching all these years... Do you suppose—"

"*What,* Bea?"

"Do you suppose it would work? Have I been blind?" She was rising slowly, as if in a dream, and the light from below showed an almost fanatical fervor coming into her mysterious eyes. "Would I get rid of this guilty traitor feeling if I'd see it his way?"

"*Who's* way?"

"Vin's. If I'd do what he wants me to do—marry him—cast my lot with him and the rest of my people—"

BILL nodded slowly. A new understanding was soaking into his dizzy brain. Vin...his friend...the swellest guy that ever lived...

"So that—that's it, is it, Bea?" All the spirit was gone out of Bill.

"I believe that's it—"

Bill's arm reached impulsively, tried to draw her back into the shadows. "Wait. Don't you want to think it over?"

"I'm going to dive down to the river, Bill, and swim over to them, tell them I've come to stay. They need me. Vin *deserves*—"

"No, Bea!" Bill leaped up. "For God's sake, not in that spirit..."

She ran along the edge of the ledge, stopped directly above the center of the river. For an instant she was the statue of the perfect woman, poised to dive.

But the sharp voice of Thork rang through the air. The meeting took a weird turn back to violence. In one brief, harsh pronouncement the ugly lieutenant threw overboard all of Vin's and the scientist's hard-won gains.

"I repeat, the horse-fish still have rights. We'll leave the girl out of this because she's a spiny-girl. And I'll swear to her innocence. But you are entitled *to a life* in exchange for these broken eggs."

The horse-fish waved their webbed hands like banners.

"Yes," Thork shouted, *"I maintain you are entitled to kill the upper-world man who committed the crime..."*

Bill caught only half a glimpse of the pandemonium. He saw George Vinson try to reach the speaker's platform. Windy Muff was helping him. And the scientist, like the other two, was shouting to the green sea-creatures to hold their places and listen.

But Vin and his party were hurled back by a gang of horse-fish waving poison scorpion fish in their faces. Bull's-Eye, the friend of the lieutenant, was leading them.

At the same moment other groups of horse-fish started chasing off in a dozen different directions.

The spiny-men themselves jumped on the bandwagon that Thork had set in motion. Their shouts filled the air: *"Bring him in!" "What can we lose!" "The horse-fish still have rights!" "Anything to keep peace!" "Bring him in!"*

Bill caught his breath. Like arms of an explosion these creatures were shooting out in all directions. The frenzy of violence was on them. They were after him.

At that instant Bea's footsteps pounded past him, her hand swished across his shoulder.

"Follow me, Bill..." she cried. Together they bounded over the arched ledge to the east. They leaped a narrow gap. Bill had the dizzy sensation of flying over a hundred-foot drop, with bright light glowing up against his silhouetted bare feet and legs.

Bea, only a few paces ahead of him, was racing with confidence. She must have remembered these trails from childhood. The toss of her dark tresses showed that she was keeping an eye on the zigzag trails. They were hardly a quarter of a mile away.

But suddenly she stopped, flinging a hand back at Bill.

The ledge ahead was blocked off. New seepage had cut off the trail since Bea, as a child, had traversed this narrow path.

"Back!" she panted, bounding ahead of him. "Keep in the shadow..."

BUT this time when they leaped over the narrow gap they heard an explosive outcry from somewhere below. The light had caught them.

They ran like wildfire now. It was a race to the west end of the passage. There, Bill remembered, they'd be able to duck through the A-shaped entrance to the dark sea cavern.

But as they chased down the incline toward the western end of the narrow ledge, they saw a cluster of webbed hands rise in their pathway. Six or seven horse-fish were scrambling up the narrow arched path carrying their poison weapons.

"Back again!" Bea shouted. And as Bill tried to jerk a stone loose from the frozen wall, she cried, "No! Come on!"

Then he was running at her side, heedless of the light. She gasped between breaths, "The fourth mound on the left, Bill... Can you make it...under water? Come on... Stay right with me..."

They glanced back when they reached the point above the center of the river. The horse-fish were hurling their weapons like hand-grenades. A poisonous lionfish rolled in the stone dust near Bill's bare feet, and its orange and black fins stiffened for action.

"Together!" Bea panted.

They dived. On the descent Bill gathered the confusion of sounds into his ears, aware that he was plunging from one danger to another. Gangs of horse-fish would see and rush back to the river. From the distance the slushing sound of the waterfall was growing stronger.

Together they plunged under for the long under-water swim. Bea cut deep, and Bill followed. For the next couple of minutes they shot straight up the central channel.

Now their ears caught the plunging of other divers. Bea forced a swifter pace. Then she suddenly plowed along an inclined channel bottom and rose. Bill followed her up through the darkness. He came up into air.

The surrounding blackness of the mud mound was relieved only by a few narrow peepholes of light. Bill caught his breath and followed Bea down again.

For five swift breathless underwater swims the chase went on. Each time they came up for a breath they could see that their pursuers were gaining ground. They could see the panting gills, the blazing little magenta eyes and savage mouths skimming beneath the surface. Here and there they caught glimpses of webbed hands clutching specimens of poisonous sea-life.

In the fifth empty mud hut they entered, Bea choked, "It's over!"

BILL heard a rush of water in the black entrance through which they had risen. The horse-fish would catch them this time. There would be no room to dart past a horse-fish in that under-water passage.

But Bill sprang up, struck his husky shoulders against the baked-mud roof. It strained, cracked. The gash of light showed the noses of horse-fish scrambling up out of the inky liquid. Bill crashed the roof again and it crumbled in a mass of debris. But he and Bea were out and on the run.

"Quick headwork!" Bea's smile flashed at him from her dirt-smeared face. It was a grim smile, aware of the nearness of death, but there was courage in it.

In the mad footrace that followed, Bill and Bea gained over the horse-fish. They rounded the upper end of the merged cities, leaping inlets, dodging pools of imprisoned scorpion fish, passing small parties of creatures that were neither horse-fish nor spiny-men but something of both.

At nearly every turn a new surprise party was awaiting them. Horse-fish were trying to close in from all directions.

But not spiny-men. Somehow their explosive violence had become disorganized and they were doing more shouting than chasing. Bill understood. They were willing to catch him; but their discovery that their own Bea-Bea was helping him race to freedom had thrown them into confusion.

Now Bea ran straight over the triple domes of the king's mud palace and jumped to the edge of the zigzagging ascent. Bill felt the mud roof break under his feet and he bounded after her. Then they were running side-by-side up the trail.

Somewhere high above there was a patch of open sky. But nearer at hand there were parties of guards from both cities.

Two hundred feet up they came to a dead stop. A semicircle of hardened guardsmen with strong human faces, slightly webbed hands, and spiny bare backs bobbed up out of the stonewall barrier, marched forth to cut off the trail from both directions.

The leader of the guards stepped over to a pink globe and inserted his head in the phone. Then he emerged and barked his orders.

"Thork says we're to hold Bea-Bea. As for the man, we're to let the horse-fish guards have their own way with him." The leader whistled a signal and twenty horse-fish, stationed a little farther up the trail, came bounding down over the rocks swinging loops of seaweed rope.

CHAPTER FOURTEEN

BILL and Bea stood on the point of a hairpin turn, watching the semicircle of guards close their ranks. An opening was left for the horse-fish to gallop through, like a band of weird cowpunchers on a rampage.

"Stay with me!"

Once again Bea's courageous whisper gave Bill his cue. Bea sprang over the edge of the trail and caught herself on a ledge twenty feet below. Then she was off again, on what seemed to be an uncharted road to sudden death. Bill followed on her heels.

He followed without looking back, though the seaweed ropes were swishing right back of him. Once a loop caught on his forehead and he barely ducked in time. If it had settled over his neck he'd have gone tumbling down the steep rocky wall, perhaps to hang himself.

This was no marked trail. Bea was fighting to catch the least perilous handholds. In places the wall was like the face of a skyscraper.

But every step brought them nearer to the bounding two hundred-foot waterfall. And now Bill guessed her strategy.

"It's our old dive, Bill!" Her eyes flashed at him. "This is where I learned it. Four swift death-leaps in succession."

Bill felt the spray of water on his bare chest and legs. Then he felt the snap of rope over his arm. The loop suddenly tightened on his wrist.

He had an instant's glimpse of the three horse-fish jerking the other end of the rope. They must have been mad to take such chances, standing on a four-foot shelf.

As they jerked, Bill dropped into the big rock basin where the vast fall of water was roaring in and out. One hand found a hold. The other was tending the rope. It gave, and he saw the three horse-fish fly out into space. Two of them slipped off and fell down—down—

No one would hear them crush to pulp. The roar of the falls would drown that sound. But the hosts of creatures below would see. Their little faces were staring up—

Jerk!

The weight of the third horse-fish couldn't have pulled the rope that hard. Bill struggled to free his wrist. Momentarily he released his handhold.

"Careful, Bill!" Bea screamed. The horse-fish that had held on had swung, pendulum style, to wedge himself safely in a crevice. There he applied the leverage of his arms to the rope, *and pulled Bill over.*

Bill saw too late. He skidded over the slippery edge of the basin and shot down with the fall.

ON the descent he barely succeeded in freeing himself of the rope. He straightened out with the falling water, fought toward what appeared to be the deepest point of the approaching pool. He struck it for a shallow dive—and was off again for the next waterfall descent.

Then another—and a fourth.

And before he had had time to catch his breath he was looking up from the boiling surface of the river to see Beatrice, with all her grace and beauty, plunge down the same succession of falls.

She bobbed up beside him. They looked back at the mountainous wall where several horse-fish guards were perched. The little green figures showed no inclination to duplicate the series of dives. Then Bill and Bea turned to face the hosts of spiny-men on the riverbank. *The crowds were cheering...*

"That's for you," Bill said. "Why don't you go back to them and stay clear of my fate?"

"Because I want to share your fate, Bill." Bea swam close to him, reached out to grip his hand. "I knew as soon as they started after you that I was wrong—about trying to stay here and be loyal, I mean. I'd rather die with you—"

The clamoring voices from the riverbank were demanding that they come. And though it was puzzling, the voices carried no tone of menace. The shouts were welcoming them, hailing them for their valiant escape, heaping verbal honors upon them.

Bill and Bea obeyed. But it was several minutes before they could understand the strange turn of events. They were made to sit down on comfortable mats and relax. And Bill found it impossible to relax with throngs of spiny-men and horse-fish crowding around.

At first everyone talked at once, but soon the talking was left to Vin, with interpolations from Windy Muff.

"I started it," Windy said. "I figured it was time for me to do a little lyin' to get you outa trouble. So I told the bunch that you wasn't the one that busted into the eggs. It was Thork. I said I'd seen him with my own eyes, and you only went in afterwards to make sure he hadn't got up in the top of the cylinder to bother Bea."

"And as we soon discovered," said Vinson, "Windy's guess was right. Yellow-Z discovered Thork's foot tracks in the egg-compartment. There was nothing for Thork to do but admit it."

"What happened to Thork?" Bill asked anxiously, catching the flicker of worry in Bea's eyes.

"We fought," said Vin. "We've always been enemies—and rivals. When he found himself caught, he turned on me.

Bull's-Eye tried to help him, but it was a mistake, because other horse-fish jumped in on my side."

Vinson paused to glance at the bruised fist of his webbed left hand.

"That's when you popped him," said Windy.

"Yes, I gave it to Thork and he took an unfortunate spill."

"Unfortunate?" said Bea.

"He fell," said Vin, "against the scorpion fish that Bull's-Eye was trying to use on me. I think he'll die before morning in spite of the care they're giving him."

THERE was a cool silence. Bill wondered what the horse-fish were thinking, after all the trouble Thork had made for them, and after all he had pretended to be the champion of their rights.

"That ain't all," said Windy. "Here comes Yellow-Z and the king now."

While the aged white-haired old spiny-man approached, the throngs rose and waited respectfully.

"You got a surprise comin', Bea," Windy whispered. "You see, when Thork fell and Bull's-Eye was crouchin' in the way, darned if the horse-fish's stabbers didn't stick the old boy right along the backbone."

"We saw it happen," said Vin, "and it gave us an idea—if Thork's inner sentiments were transferred to Bull's-Eye, we could put the horse-fish into a thought-phone and pick up Thork's dying thoughts. So we did."

"And guess what—"

But the king was entering the circle now, and everyone was silent. Maribeau, the scientist, crowded close to miss no detail of the impromptu ceremony. Windy's eyes ran rings around the breathless audience. Bea's shoulder trembled against Bill's arm.

"I have been asked to approve the revelation," said the king in a low rumbling voice, "which one of the horse-fish has made of Thork's dying sentiments. Those sentiments, as quoted to me are, 'They mustn't know that Bea-Bea is *not* a spiny-girl. They mustn't know that I stole her from an English family visiting from above—' "

"Thork said that?" Bea said, jumping up in astonishment.

"That, as caught by Bull's-Eye," said the king, "was Thork's secret thought immediately after the mortal wound struck him. And I must add—"

Bill could hear Bea's heart pounding.

"...that the lieutenant confided this secret to me many years ago," the king said calmly. "It happened after the drowning of one of our babies...so I assure you, Bea, that you are not a spiny-girl."

Bea nearly fainted as Bill helped her gently to her seat. A strange fire lit up her eyes, and with burning amazement she looked from Bill to Vin and back to Bill. A curious smile touched the corners of her lips, as if she were laughing inside.

"But perhaps," the king added, after he had turned to go, "we should insist that you *are* a spiny-girl, since we've raised you. That, however, I shall leave with our mediator and new lieutenant, Vin-Vin."

The white haired king hobbled away.

Vin turned to Bea and Bill, smiling. "Friends, my yacht and sailors are up there—at your service. Will you come back sometime?"

"Will we!" Bill said it enthusiastically. Then he turned to Bea. "Will we?"

"We'll think it over, Vin." Bea smiled. "After all that you and the scientist have told us, we may want to come—to live—for the benefit of our descendants."

THE END

If you've enjoyed this book, you will not want to miss these terrific titles…

ARMCHAIR SCI-FI, FANTASY, & HORROR DOUBLE NOVELS, $12.95 each

D-81 **THE LAST PLEA** by Robert Bloch
OMEGA by Robert Sheckley

D-82 **WOMAN FROM ANOTHER PLANET** by Frank Belknap Long
HOMECALLING by Judith Merril

D-83 **WHEN TWO WORLDS MEET** by Robert Moore Williams
THE MAN WHO HAD NO BRAINS by Jeff Sutton

D-84 **THE SPECTRE OF SUICIDE SWAMP** by E. K. Jarvis
IT'S MAGIC, YOU DOPE! by Jack Sharkey

D-85 **THE STARSHIP FROM SIRIUS** by Rog Phillips
FINAL WEAPON by Everett Cole

D-86 **TREASURE ON THUNDER MOON** by Edmond Hamilton
TRAIL OF THE ASTROGAR by Henry Haase

D-87 **VENGEANCE OF KYVOR** by Randall Garrett
AT THE EARTH'S CORE by Edgar Rice Burroughs

D-88 **THE MAD ROBOT** by William P. McGivern
THE RUNNING MAN by J. Holly Hunter

D-89 **THE WOMAN IN SKIN 13** by Paul W. Fairman
THE VENUS ENIGMA by Joe Gibson

D-90 **DWELLERS OF THE DEEP** by Don Wilcox
NIGHT OF THE LONG KNIVES by Fritz Leiber

ARMCHAIR SCIENCE FICTION CLASSICS, $12.95 each

C-28 **THE MAN FROM TOMORROW**
by Stanton A. Coblentz

C-29 **THE GREEN MAN OF GRAYPEC**
by Festus Pragnell

C-30 **THE SHAVER MYSTERY, Book Four**
by Richard S. Shaver

ARMCHAIR MASTERS OF SCIENCE FICTION SERIES, $16.95 each

MS-7 **MASTERS OF SCIENCE FICTION AND FANTASY, Vol. Seven**
Lester del Rey, "The Band Played On" and other tales

MS-8 **MASTERS OF SCIENCE FICTION, Vol. Eight**
Milton Lesser, "'A' is for Android" and other tales

AN UNPLEASANT VISION
OF THE FUTURE...

It was a grim place indeed. Earth was now a horrifying post-apocalyptic world where fate could be cruel and life was often very short. Every man struggled mightily to survive from one day to the next and often the only real protection lay in one's ability to make quick, unhesitating use of a knife or a gun.

In this forlorn world, three drifters came together in a life-starved area known only as "the Deathlands," where multi-colored radioactive dust was often too much in evidence. However, when the three stumbled across a crashed plane and its pilot, there suddenly seemed to be a light of hope. Could the plane be repaired? Was there a chance of freedom from the radioactive wastelands that trapped them?

ABOUT FRITZ LEIBER:

Fritz Leiber was born in Chicago, Illinois on December 24 [th], 1910. His parents (Fritz, Sr. and Virginia) had a very st rong theatrical background, being part of a long-touring Shakespearean troupe.

As a teenager, Fritz, Jr . studied philosophy at the University of Chica go. He later toured as an actor with his parents' acting company, Fritz Leiber & Co.

Not bound by the pull of his parents' acting careers, Fritz eventually became a t op-flight sci-fi and fantasy writer. His first publishe d wor k was *Two Sought Adventure*, which was published in *Unknown* in 1939. Leiber was initially much influenced by H. P. Lovecraft and wrote numerous Cthulhu Mythos tales. Later works included two notable novels, *Conjure Wife* (1943) and *The Wanderer* (1964) the latter of which won the Hugo award for bes t novel. Leiber wrote countless other novels and s hort stories, but his career suffered at times due to bouts with alcoholism, including a "lost" three-year period in the late '60s and early '70s.

Writing top-notch science fiction and fantasy was not, however, the only field Fritz Leiber excelled in; he became an expert fencer, a poet, an actor on stage and in movies, and a champion chess player. His greatest accomplishment in the world of chess was taking first place honors in the 1958 Santa Monica Open Chess Championship.

After a long, sometimes tumultuous, but often distinguished career, whic h inc luding the winning of numerous Hugo and Nebula aw ards, Fritz Leiber died on September 5th, 1992 at the age of 81.

NIGHT OF THE LONG KNIVES

By
FRITZ LEIBER

ARMCHAIR FICTION
PO Box 4369, Medford, Oregon   97501-0168

*For more information about Armchair Books and products, visit our
website at…*

www.armchairfiction.com

Or email us at…

armchairfiction@yahoo.com

CHAPTER ONE

Any man who saw you, or even heard your footsteps must be ambushed,
stalked and killed, whether needed for food or not. Otherwise, so long as
his strength held out, he would be on your trail.
—The Twenty-Fifth Hour,
by Herbert Best

I was one hundred miles from Nowhere—and I mean that
literally—when I spotted this girl out of the corner of my eye.
I'd been keeping an extra lookout because I still expected the
other undead bugger left over from the murder party at
Nowhere to be stalking me.

I'd been following a line of high-voltage towers all canted
over at the same gentlemanly tipsy angle by an old blast from
the Last War. I judged the girl was going in the same general
direction and was being edged over toward my course by a
drift of dust that even at my distance showed dangerous
metallic gleams and dark humps that might be dead men or
cattle.

She looked slim, dark topped, and on guard. Small like me
and like me wearing a scarf loosely around the lower half of
her face in the style of the old buckaroos.

We didn't wave or turn our heads or give the slightest
indication we'd seen each other as our paths slowly
converged. But we were intensely, minutely watchful—I
knew I was and she had better be.

Overhead the sky was a low dust haze, as always. I don't
remember what a high sky looks like. Three years ago I think
I saw Venus. Or it may have been Sirius or Jupiter.

The hot smoky light was turning from the amber of midday to the bloody bronze of evening.

The line of towers I was following showed the faintest spread in the direction of their canting—they must have been only a few miles from blast center. As I passed each one I could see where the metal on the blast side had been eroded—vaporized by the original blast, mostly smoothly, but with welts and pustules where the metal had merely melted and run. I supposed the lines the towers carried had all been vaporized too, but with the haze I couldn't be sure, though I did see three dark blobs up there that might be vultures perching.

From the drift around the foot of the nearest tower a human skull peered whitely. That is rather unusual. Years later now you still see more dead bodies with the meat on them than skeletons. Intense radiation has killed their bacteria and preserved them indefinitely from decay, just like the packaged meat in the last advertisements. In fact such bodies are one of the signs of a really hot drift—you avoid them. The vultures pass up such poisonously hot carrion too—they've learned their lesson.

Ahead some big gas tanks began to loom up, like deformed battleships and flat-tops in a smoke screen, their prows being the juncture of the natural curve of the off-blast side with the massive concavity of the on-blast side.

None of the three other buggers and me had had too clear an idea of where Nowhere had been—hence, in part, the name—but I knew in a general way that I was somewhere in the Deathlands between Porter County and Ouachita Parish, probably much nearer the former.

It's a real mixed-up America we've got these days, you know, with just the faintest trickle of a sense of identity left, like a guy in the paddedest cell in the most locked up ward in the whole loony bin. If a time traveler from mid Twentieth

Century hopped forward to it across the few intervening years and looked at a map of it, if anybody has a map of it, he'd think that the map had run—that it had got some sort of disease that had swollen a few tiny parts beyond all bounds, paper tumors, while most of the other parts, the parts he remembered carrying names in such big print and showing such bold colors, had shrunk to nothingness.

To the east he'd see Atlantic Highlands and Savannah Fortress. To the west, Walla Walla Territory, Pacific Palisades, and Los Alamos—and there he'd see an actual change in the coastline, I'm told, where three of the biggest stockpiles of fusionables let go and opened Death Valley to the sea—so that Los Alamos is closer to being a port. Centrally he'd find Porter County and Manteno Asylum surprisingly close together near the Great Lakes, which are tilted and spilled out a bit toward the southwest with the big quake. South-centrally: Ouachita Parish inching up the Mississippi from old Louisiana under the cruel urging of the Fisher Sheriffs.

Those he'd find and a few, a very few other places, including a couple I suppose I haven't heard of. Practically all of them would surprise him—no one can predict what scraps of a blasted nation are going to hang onto a shred of organization and ruthlessly maintain it and very slowly and very jealously extend it.

But biggest of all, occupying practically all the map, reducing all those swollen localities I've mentioned back to tiny blobs, bounding most of America and thrusting its jetty pseudopods everywhere, he'd see the great inkblot of the Deathlands. I don't know how else than by an area of solid, absolutely unrelieved black you'd represent the Deathlands with its multicolored radioactive dusts and its skimpy freightage of lonely Deathlanders, each bound on his murderous, utterly pointless, but utterly absorbing business—

an area where names like Nowhere, It, Anywhere, and the Place are the most natural thing in the world when a few of us decide to try to pad down together for a few nervous months or weeks.

As I say, I was somewhere in the Deathlands near Manteno Asylum.

The girl and me were getting closer now, well within pistol or dart range though beyond any but the most expert or lucky knife throw. She wore boots and a weathered long-sleeved shirt and jeans. The black topping was hair, piled high in an elaborate coiffure that was held in place by twisted shavings of bright metal. A fine bug-trap, I told myself.

In her left hand, which was closest to me, she carried a dart gun, pointed away from me, across her body. It was the kind of potent tiny crossbow you can't easily tell whether the spring is loaded. Back around on her left hip a small leather satchel was strapped to her belt. Also on the same side were two sheathed knives, one of which was an oddity—it had no handle, just the bare tang. For nothing but throwing, I guessed.

I let my own left hand drift a little closer to my Banker's Special in its open holster—Ray Baker's great psychological weapon, though (who knows?) the two .38 cartridges it contained might actually fire. The one I'd put to the test at Nowhere had, and very lucky for me.

She seemed to be hiding her right arm from me. Then I spotted the weapon it held, one you don't often see, a stevedore's hook. She *was* hiding her right hand, all right, she had the long sleeve pulled down over it so just the hook stuck out. I asked myself if the hand were perhaps covered with radiation scars or sores or otherwise disfigured. We Deathlanders have our vanities. I'm sensitive about my baldness.

Then she let her right arm swing more freely and I saw how short it was. She had no right hand. The hook was attached to the wrist stump.

I judged she was about ten years younger than me. I'm pushing forty, I think, though some people have judged I'm younger. No way of my knowing for sure. In this life you forget trifles like chronology.

Anyway, the age difference meant she would have quicker reflexes. I'd have to keep that in mind.

The greenishly glinting dust drift that I'd judged she was avoiding swung closer ahead. The girl's left elbow gave a little kick to the satchel on her hip and there was a sudden burst of irregular ticks that almost made me start. I steadied myself and concentrated on thinking whether I should attach any special significance to her carrying a Geiger counter. Naturally it wasn't the sort of thinking that interfered in any way with my watchfulness—you quickly lose the habit of that kind of thinking in the Deathlands or you lose something else.

It could mean she was some sort of greenhorn. Most of us old-timers can visually judge the heat of a dust drift or crater or rayed area more reliably than any instrument. Some buggers claim they just feel it, though I've never known any of the latter too eager to navigate in unfamiliar country at night—which you'd think they'd be willing to do if they could feel heat blind.

But she didn't look one bit like a tenderfoot—like for instance some citizeness newly banished from Manteno. Or like some Porter burgher's unfaithful wife or troublesome girlfriend whom he'd personally carted out beyond the ridges of cleaned-out hot dust that help guard such places, and then abandoned in revenge or from boredom—and they call themselves civilized, those cultural queers!

No, she looked like she *belonged* in the Deathlands. But then why the counter?

Her eyes might be bad, real bad. I didn't think so. She raised her boot an extra inch to step over a little jagged fragment of concrete. No.

Maybe she was just a born double-checker, using science to back up knowledge based on experience as rich as my own or richer. I've met the super-careful type before. They mostly get along pretty well, but they tend to be a shade too slow in the clutches.

Maybe she was *testing* the counter, planning to use it some other way or trade it for something.

Maybe she made a practice of traveling by night! Then the counter made good sense. But then why use it by day? Why reveal it to me in any case?

Was she trying to convince me that she was a greenhorn? Or had she hoped that the sudden noise would throw me off guard? But who would go to the trouble of carrying a Geiger counter for such devious purposes? And wouldn't she have waited until we got closer before trying the noise gambit?

Think-shmink—it gets you nowhere!

She kicked off the counter with another bump of her elbow and started to edge in toward me faster. I turned the thinking all off and gave my whole mind to watchfulness.

Soon we were barely more than eight feet apart, almost within lunging range without even the preliminary one-two step, and still we hadn't spoken or looked straight at each other, though being that close we'd had to cant our heads around a bit to keep each other in peripheral vision. Our eyes would be on each other steadily for five or six seconds, then dart forward an instant to check for rocks and holes in the trail we were following in parallel. A cultural queer from one of the "civilized" places would have found it funny, I suppose, if he'd been able to watch us perform in an arena or from behind armor glass for his exclusive pleasure.

The girl had eyebrows as black as her hair, which in its piled-up and metal-knotted savagery called to mind African queens despite her typical pale complexion—very little ultraviolet gets through the dust. From the inside corner of her right eye socket a narrow radiation scar ran up between her eyebrows and across her forehead at a rakish angle until it disappeared under a sweep of hair at the upper left corner of her forehead.

I'd been smelling her, of course, for some time.

I could even tell the color of her eyes now. They were blue. It's a color you never see. Almost no dusts have a bluish cast, there are few blue objects except certain dark steels, the sky never gets very far away from the orange range, though it is green from time to time, and water reflects the sky.

Yes, she had blue eyes, blue eyes and that jaunty scar, blue eyes and that jaunty scar and a dart gun and a steel hook for a right hand, and we were walking side by side, eight feet apart, not an inch closer, still not looking straight at each other, still not saying a word, and I realized that the initial period of unadulterated watchfulness was over, that I'd had adequate opportunity to inspect this girl and size her up, and that night was coming on fast, and that here I was, once again, back with *the problem of the two urges.*

I could try either to kill her or go to bed with her.

I know that at this point the cultural queers (and certainly our imaginary time traveler from mid Twentieth Century) would make a great noise about not understanding and not believing in the genuineness of the simple urge to murder that governs the lives of us Deathlanders. Like detective-story pundits, they would say that a man or woman murders for gain, or concealment of crime, or from thwarted sexual desire or outraged sexual possessiveness—and maybe they would list a few other "rational" motives—but not, they would say, just for the simple sake of murder, for the sure release and relief it gives, for the sake of wiping out one recognizable bit more (the closest bit we can, since those of us with the courage or lazy rationality to wipe out ourselves have long since done so)—wiping out one recognizable bit more of the whole miserable, unutterably disgusting human mess. Unless, they would say, a person is completely insane, which is actually how all outsiders view us Deathlanders. They can think of us in no other way.

I guess cultural queers and time travelers simply *don't* understand, though to be so blind it seems to me that they have to overlook much of the history of the Last War and of the subsequent years, especially the mushrooming of crackpot cults with a murder tinge: the werewolf gangs, the Berserkers and Amuckers, the revival of Shiva worship and the Black Mass, the machine wreckers, the kill-the-killers movements, the new witchcraft, the Unholy Creepers, the Unconsciousers, the radioactive blue gods and rocket devils of the Atomites, and a dozen other groupings clearly prefiguring Deathlander psychology. Those cults had all been as unpredictable as Thuggee or the Dancing Madness of the Middle Ages or the Children's Crusade, yet they had happened just the same.

But cultural queers are good at overlooking things. They have to be, I suppose. They think they're humanity growing again. Yes, despite their laughable warpedness and hysterical crippledness, they actually believe—each howlingly different community of them—that they're the new Adams and Eves. They're all excited about themselves and whether or not they wear fig leaves. They don't carry with them, twenty-four hours a day, like us Deathlanders do, the burden of all that was forever lost.

Since I've gone this far I'll go a bit further and make the paradoxical admission that even us Deathlanders don't really understand our urge to murder. Oh, we have our rationalizations of it, just like everyone has of his ruling passion—we call ourselves junkmen, scavengers, gangrene surgeons; we sometimes believe we're doing the person we kill the ultimate kindness, yes and get slobbery tearful about it afterwards; we sometimes tell ourselves we've finally found and are rubbing out the one man or woman who was responsible for everything; we talk, mostly to ourselves, about the aesthetics of homicide; we occasionally admit, but only each to himself alone, that we're just plain nuts.

But we don't really understand our urge to murder, we only *feel* it.

At the hateful sight of another human being, we feel it begins to grow in us until it becomes an overpowering impulse that jerks us, like a puppet is jerked by its strings, into the act itself or its attempted commission.

Like I was feeling it grow in me now as we did this parallel deathmarch through the reddening haze, me and this girl and our problem. This girl with the blue eyes and the jaunty scar.

The problem of the *two* urges, I said. The other urge, the sexual, is one that I know all cultural queers (and certainly our time traveler) would claim to know all about. Maybe they do. But I wonder if they understand how intense it can be with us Deathlanders when it's the only release (except maybe liquor and drugs, which we seldom can get and even more rarely dare use)—the only complete release, even though a brief one, from the overpowering loneliness and from the tyranny of the urge to kill.

To embrace, to possess, to glut lust on, yes even briefly to love, briefly to shelter in—that was good, that was a relief and release to be treasured.

But it couldn't last. You could draw it out, prop it up perhaps for a few days, for a month even (though sometimes not for a single night)—you might even start to talk to each other a little, after a while—but it could never last. The glands always tire, if nothing else.

Murder was the only *final* solution, the only *permanent* release. Only us Deathlanders know how good it feels. But then after the kill the loneliness would come back, redoubled, and after a while I'd meet another hateful human...

Our problem of the two urges. As I watched this girl slogging along parallel to me, as I kept constant watch on her of course, I wondered how *she* was feeling the two urges. Was she attracted to the ridgy scars on my cheeks half revealed by my scarf?—to me they have a pleasing symmetry. Was she wondering how my head and face looked without the black felt skullcap low-visored over my eyes? Or was she thinking mostly of that hook swinging into my throat under the chin and dragging me down?

I couldn't tell. She looked as poker-faced as I was trying to.

For that matter, I asked myself, how was *I* feeling the two urges?—how was I feeling them as I watched this girl with the blue eyes and the jaunty scar and the arrogantly thinned lips that asked to be smashed, and the slender throat?—and I realized that there was no way to describe that, not even to myself. I could only feel the two urges grow in me, side by side, like monstrous twins, until they would simply be too big for my taut body and one of them would have to get out fast.

I don't know which one of us started to slow down first, it happened so gradually, but the dust puffs that rise from the ground of the Deathlands under even the lightest treading became smaller and smaller around our steps and finally vanished altogether, and we were standing still. Only then did I notice the obvious physical trigger for our stopping. An old freeway ran at right angles across our path. The shoulder by which we'd approached it was sharply eroded, so that the pavement, which even had a shallow cave eroded under it, was a good three feet above the level of our path, forming a low wall. From where I'd stopped I could almost reach out and touch the rough-edged smooth-topped concrete. So could she.

We were right in the midst of the gas tanks now, six or seven of them towered around us, squeezed like beer cans by the decade-old blast but their metal looking sound enough until you became aware of the red light showing through in odd patterns of dots and dashes where vaporization or later erosion had been complete. Almost but not quite lace-work. Just ahead of us, right across the freeway, was the six-storey skeletal structure of an old cracking plant, sagged like the power towers away from the blast and the lower storeys drifted with piles and ridges and smooth gobbets of dust.

The light was getting redder and smokier every minute.

With the cessation of the physical movement of walking, which is always some sort of release for emotions, I could feel the twin urges growing faster in me. But that was all right, I told myself—this was the crisis, as she must realize too, and that should key us up to bear the urges a little longer without explosion.

I was the first to start to turn my head. For the first time I looked straight into her eyes and she into mine. And as always happens at such times, a third urge appeared abruptly, an urge momentarily as strong as the other two—the urge to speak, to tell and ask all about it. But even as I started to phrase the first crazily happy greeting, my throat lumped, as I'd known it would, with the awful melancholy of all that was forever lost, with the uselessness of any communication, with the impossibility of recreating the past, our individual pasts, any pasts. And as it always does, the third urge died.

I could tell she was feeling that ultimate pain just like me. I could see her eyelids squeeze down on her eyes and her face lift and her shoulders go back as she swallowed hard.

She was the first to start to lay aside a weapon. She took two sidewise steps toward the freeway and reached her whole left arm further across her body and laid the dart gun on the concrete and drew back her hand from it about six inches. At the same time looking at me hard—fiercely angrily, you'd say—across her left shoulder. She had the experienced duelist's trick of seeming to look into my eyes but actually focussing on my mouth. I was using the same gimmick myself—it's tiring to look straight into another person's eyes and it can put you off guard.

My left side was nearest the wall so I didn't for the moment have the problem of reaching across my body. I took the same sidewise steps she had and using just two fingers, very gingerly—*disarmingly*, I hoped—I lifted my antique firearm from its holster and laid it on the concrete and drew back my hand from it all the way. Now it was up to her again, or should be. Her hook was going to be quite a problem, I realized, but we needn't come to it right away.

She temporized by successively unsheathing the two knives at her left side and laying them beside the dart gun. Then she stopped and her look told me plainly that it was up to me.

Now I am a bugger who believes in carrying *one perfect knife*—otherwise, I know for a fact, you'll go knife-happy and end up by weighing yourself down with dozens, literally. So I am naturally very reluctant to get out of touch in any way with Mother, who is a little rusty along the sides but made of the toughest and most sharpenable alloy steel I've ever run across.

Still, I was most curious to find out what she'd do about that hook, so I finally laid Mother on the concrete beside the

.38 and rested my hands lightly on my hips, all ready to enjoy myself—at least I hoped I gave that impression.

She smiled, it was almost a nice smile—by now we'd let our scarves drop since we weren't raising any more dust—and then she took hold of the hook with her left hand and started to unscrew it from the leather-and-metal base fitting over her stump.

Of course, I told myself. And her second knife, the one without a grip, must be that way so she could screw its tang into the base when she wanted a knife on her right hand instead of a hook. I ought to have guessed.

I grinned my admiration of her mechanical ingenuity and immediately unhitched my knapsack and laid it beside my weapons. Then a thought occurred to me. I opened the knapsack and moving my hand slowly and very openly so she'd have no reason to suspect a ruse, I drew out a blanket and, trying to show her both sides of it in the process, as if I were performing some damned conjuring trick, dropped it gently on the ground between us.

She unsnapped the straps on her satchel that fastened it to her belt and laid it aside and then she took off her belt too, slowly drawing it through the wide loops of weathered denim. Then she looked meaningfully at my belt.

I had to agree with her. Belts, especially heavy-buckled ones like ours, can be nasty weapons. I removed mine. Simultaneously each belt joined its corresponding pile of weapons and other belongings.

She shook her head, not in any sort of negation, and ran her fingers into the black hair at several points, to show me it hid no weapon, then looked at me questioningly. I nodded that I was satisfied—I hadn't seen anything run out of it, by the way. Then she looked up at my black skullcap and she raised her eyebrows and smiled again, this time with a spice of mocking anticipation.

In some ways I hate to part with that headpiece more than I do with Mother. Not really because of its sandwiched lead-mesh inner lining—if the rays haven't baked my brain yet they never will and I'm sure that the patches of lead mesh sewed into my pants over my loins give a lot more practical protection. But I was getting real attracted to this girl by now and there are times when a person must make a sacrifice of his vanity. I whipped off my stylish black felt and tossed it on my pile and dared her to laugh at my shiny egg top.

Strangely she didn't even smile. She parted her lips and ran her tongue along the upper one. I gave an eager grin in reply, an incautiously wide one, and she saw my plates flash.

My plates are something rather special though they are by no means unique. Back toward the end of the Last War, when it was obvious to any realist how bad things were going to be, though not how strangely terrible, a number of people, like myself, had all their teeth jerked and replaced with durable plates. I went some of them one better. My plates were stainless steel biting and chewing ridges, smooth continuous ones that didn't attempt to copy individual teeth. A person who looks closely at a slab of chewing tobacco, say, I offer him will be puzzled by the smoothly curved incision, made as if by a razor blade mounted on the arm of a compass. Magnetic powder buried in my gums makes for a real nice fit.

This sacrifice was worse than my hat and Mother combined, but I could see the girl expected me to make it and would take no substitutes, and in this attitude I had to admit that she showed very sound judgment, because I keep the incisor parts of those plates filed to razor sharpness. I have to be careful about my tongue and lips but I figure it's worth it. With my dental scimitars I can in a wink bite out a chunk of throat and windpipe or jugular, though I've never had occasion to do so yet.

For the first minute it made me feel like an old man, a real dodderer, but by now the attraction this girl had for me was getting irrational. I carefully laid the two plates on top of my knapsack.

In return, as a sort of reward you might say, she opened her mouth wide and showed me what was left of her own teeth—about two-thirds of them, a patchwork of tartar and gold.

We took off our boots, pants and shirts, she watching very suspiciously—I knew she'd been skeptical of my carrying only one knife.

Oddly perhaps, considering how touchy I am about my baldness, I felt no sensitivity about revealing the lack of hair on my chest and in fact a sort of pride in displaying the slanting radiation scars that have replaced it, though they are crawling keloids of the ugliest, bumpiest sort. I guess to me such scars are tribal insignia—one-man and one-woman tribes of course. No question but that the scar on the girl's forehead had been the first focus of my desire for her and it still added to my interest.

By now we weren't staying as perfectly on guard or watching each other's clothing for concealed weapons as carefully as we should—I know I wasn't. It was getting dark fast, there wasn't much time left, and the other interest was simply becoming too great.

We were still automatically careful about how we did things. For instance the way we took off our pants was like ballet, simultaneously crouching a little on the left foot and whipping the right leg out of its sheath in one movement, all ready to jump without tripping ourselves if the other person did anything funny, and then skinning down the left pants-leg with a movement almost as swift.

But as I say it was getting too late for perfect watchfulness, in fact for any kind of effective watchfulness at all. The complexion of the whole situation was changing in a rush. The possibilities of dealing or receiving death—along with the chance of the minor indignity of cannibalism, which some of us practice—were suddenly gone, all gone. It was going to be all right this time, I was telling myself. This was the time it would be different, this was the time love would last, this was the time lust would be the firm foundation for understanding and trust, this time there would be really safe sleeping. This girl's body would be home for me, a beautiful tender inexhaustibly exciting home, and mine for her, for always.

As she threw off her shirt, the last darkly red light showed me another smooth slantwise scar, this one around her hips, like a narrow girdle that has slipped down a little on one side.

CHAPTER TWO

Murder most foul, as in the best it is;
But this most foul, strange and unnatural.
—Hamlet

When I woke the light was almost full amber and I could feel no flesh against mine, only the blanket under me. I very slowly rolled over and there she was, sitting on the corner of the blanket not two feet from me, combing her long black hair with a big, wide-toothed comb she'd screwed into the leather-and-metal cap over her wrist stump.

She'd put on her pants and shirt, but the former were rolled up to her knees and the latter, though tucked in, wasn't buttoned.

She was looking at me, contemplating me you might say, quite dreamily but with a faint, easy smile.

I smiled back at her.

It was lovely.

Too lovely. There had to be something wrong with it.

There was. Oh, nothing big. Just a solitary trifle—
nothing worth noticing really.

But the tiniest solitary things can sometimes be the most
irritating, like *one* mosquito.

When I'd first rolled over she'd been combing her hair
straight back, revealing a wedge of baldness following the
continuation of her forehead scar deep back across her scalp.
Now with a movement that was swift though not hurried-
looking she swept the mass of her hair forward and to the
left, so that it covered the bald area. Also her lips
straightened out.

I was hurt. She shouldn't have hidden her bit of baldness,
it was something we had in common, something that brought
us closer. And she shouldn't have stopped smiling at just that
moment. Didn't she realize I loved that blaze on her scalp
just as much as any other part of her, that she no longer had
any need to practice vanity in front of me?

Didn't she realize that as soon as she stopped smiling, her
contemplative stare became an insult to me? What right had
she to stare, critically I felt sure, at my bald head? What right
had she to know about the nearly-healed ulcer on my left
shin?—that was a piece of information worth a man's life in a
fight. What right had she to cover up, anyways, while I was
still naked? She ought to have waked me up so that we could
have got dressed as we'd undressed, together. There were
lots of things wrong with her manners.

Oh, I know that if I'd been able to think calmly, maybe if
I'd just had some breakfast or a little coffee inside me, or
even if there'd been some hot breakfast to eat at that
moment, I'd have recognized my irritation for the irrational,
one-mosquito surge of negative feeling that it was.

Even without breakfast, if I'd just had the knowledge that
there was a reasonably secure day ahead of me in which
there'd be an opportunity for me to straighten out my

feelings, I wouldn't have been irked, or at least being irked wouldn't have bothered me terribly.

But a sense of security is an even rarer commodity in the Deathlands than a hot breakfast.

Given just the ghost of a sense of security and/or some hot breakfast, I'd have told myself that she was merely being amusingly coquettish about her bald streak and her hair, that it was natural for a woman to try to preserve some mystery about herself in front of the man she beds with.

But you get leery of any kind of mystery in the Deathlands. It makes you frightened and angry, like it does an animal. Mystery is for cultural queers, strictly. The only way for two people to get along together in the Deathlands, even for a while, is never to hide anything and never to make a move that doesn't have an immediate clear explanation. You can't talk, you see, certainly not at first, and so you can't explain anything (most explanations are just lies and dreams, anyway), so you have to be doubly careful and explicit about everything you do.

This girl wasn't being either. Right now, on top of her other gaucheries, she was unscrewing the comb from her wrist—an unfriendly if not quite a hostile act, as anyone must admit.

Understand, please, I wasn't *showing* any of these negative reactions of mine any more than she was showing hers, except for her stopping smiling. In fact I *hadn't* stopped smiling, I was playing the game to the hilt.

But inside me everything was stewed up and the other urge had come back and presently it would begin to grow again. That's the trouble, you know, with sex as a solution to the problem of the two urges. It's fine while it lasts but it wears itself out and then you're back with Urge Number One and you have nothing left to balance it with.

Oh, I wouldn't kill this girl today, I probably wouldn't seriously think of killing her for a month or more, but Old Urge Number One would be there and growing, mostly under cover, all the time. Of course there were things I could do to slow its growth, lots of little gimmicks, in fact—I was pretty experienced at this business.

For instance, I could take a shot at talking to her pretty soon. For a catchy starter, I could tell her about Nowhere, how these five other buggers and me found ourselves independently skulking along after this scavenging expedition from Porter, how we naturally joined forces in that situation, how we set a pitfall for their alky-powered jeep and wrecked it and them, how when our haul turned out to be unexpectedly big the four of us left from the kill chummied up and padded down together and amused each other for a while and played games, you might say. Why, at one point we even had an old crank phonograph going and read some books. And, of course, how when the loot gave out and the fun wore off, we had our murder party and I survived along with, I think, a bugger named Jerry—at any rate, he was gone when the blood stopped spurting, and I'd had no stomach for tracking him, though I probably should have.

And in return she could tell me how she had killed off her last set of girlfriends, or boyfriends, or friend, or whatever it was.

After that, we could have a go at exchanging news, rumors and speculations about local, national and world events. Was it true that Atlantic Highlands had planes of some sort or were they from Europe? Were they actually crucifying the Deathlanders around Walla Walla or only nailing up their dead bodies as dire warnings to others such? Had Manteno made Christianity compulsory yet, or were they still tolerating Zen Buddhists? Was it true that Los Alamos had been completely wiped out by plague, but the area taboo to

Deathlanders because of the robot guards they'd left behind—metal guards eight feet tall who tramped across the white sands, wailing? Did they still have free love in Pacific Palisades? Did she know there'd been a pitched battle fought by expeditionary forces from Ouachita and Savannah Fortress? Over the loot of Birmingham, apparently, after yellow fever had finished off that principality. Had she rooted out any "observers" lately?—some of the "civilized" communities, the more "scientific" ones, try to maintain a few weather stations and the like in the Deathlands, camouflaging them elaborately and manning them with one or two impudent characters to whom we give a hard time if we uncover them. Had she heard the tale that was going around that South America and the French Riviera had survived the Last War absolutely untouched?—and the obviously ridiculous rider that they had blue skies there and saw stars every third night? Did she think that subsequent conditions were showing that the Earth actually had plunged into an interstellar dust cloud coincidentally with the start of the Last War (the dust cloud used as a cover for the first attacks, some said) or did she still hold with the majority that the dust was solely of atomic origin with a little help from volcanoes and dry spells? How many green sunsets had she seen in the last year?

After we'd chewed over those racy topics and some more like them, and incidentally got bored with guessing and fabricating, we might, if we felt especially daring and conversation were going particularly well, even take a chance on talking a little about our childhoods, about how things were before the Last War (though she was almost too young for that)—about the *little* things we remembered—the big things were much too dangerous topics to venture on and sometimes even the little memories could suddenly twist you up as if you'd swallowed lye.

But after that there wouldn't be anything left to talk about. Anything you'd risk talking about, that is. For instance, no matter how long we talked, it was very unlikely that we'd either of us tell the other anything complete or very accurate about how we lived from day to day, about our techniques of surviving and staying sane or at least functional—that would be too imprudent, it would go too much against the grain of any player of the murder game. Would I tell her, or anyone, about how I worked the ruses of playing dead and disguising myself as a woman, about my trick of picking a path just before dark and then circling back to it by a pre-surveyed route, about the chess games I played with myself, about the bottle of green, terribly hot-looking powder I carried to sprinkle behind me to bluff off pursuers? A fat chance of my revealing things like that!

And when all the talk was over, what would it have gained us? Our minds would be filled with a lot of painful stuff better kept buried—meaningless hopes, scraps of vicarious living in "cultured" communities, memories that were nothing but melancholy given concrete form. The melancholy is easiest to bear when it's the diffused background for everything; and all garbage is best kept in the can. Oh yes, our talking would have gained us a few more days of infatuation, of phantom security, but those we could have—almost as many of them, at any rate—without talking.

For instance things were smoothing over already between her and me again and I no longer felt quite so irked. She'd replaced the comb with an inoffensive-looking pair of light pliers and was doing up her hair with the metal shavings. And I was acting as if content to watch her, as in a way I was. I'd still made no move to get dressed.

She looked real sweet, you know, primping herself that way. Her face was a little flat, but it was young, and the scar gave it just the fillip it needed.

But what was going on behind that forehead right now, I asked myself? I felt real psychic this morning, my mind as clear as a bottle of White Rock you find miraculously unbroken in a blasted tavern, and the answers to the question I'd asked myself came effortlessly.

She was telling herself she'd got herself a man again, a man who was adequate in the primal clutch (I gave myself that pat on the back), and that she wouldn't have to be plagued and have her safety endangered by *that* kind of mind-dulling restlessness and yearning for a while.

She was lightly playing around with ideas about how she'd found a home and a protector, knowing she was kidding herself, that it was the most gimcracky feminine make-believe, but enjoying it just the same.

She was sizing me up, deciding in detail just what I went for in a woman, what whetted my interest, so she could keep that roused as long as seemed desirable or prudent to her to continue our relation.

She was kicking herself, only lightly to begin with, because she hadn't taken any precautions—because we who've escaped hot death against all reasonable expectations by virtue of some incalculable resistance to the ills of radioactivity, quite often find we've escaped sterility too. If she should become pregnant, she was telling herself, then she had a real sticky business ahead of her where no man could be trusted for a second.

And because she was thinking of this and because she was obviously a realistic Deathlander, she was reminding herself that a woman is basically less impulsive and daring and resourceful than a man and so had always better be sure she gets in the first blow. She would be thinking that I was a realist myself and a smart man, one able to understand her predicament quite clearly—and because of that a much sooner danger to her. She was feeling Old Number One

Urge starting to grow in her again and wondering whether it mightn't be wisest to give it the hot-house treatment.

That is the trouble with a clear mind. For a little while you see things as they really are and you can accurately predict how they're going to shape the future…and then suddenly you realize you've predicted yourself a week or a month into the future and you can't live the intervening time any more because you've already imagined it in detail. People who live in communities, even the cultural queers of our maimed era, aren't much bothered by it—there must be some sort of blinkers they hand you out along with the key to the city—but in the Deathlands it's a fairly common phenomenon and there's no hiding from it.

Me and my clear mind!—once again it had done me out of days of fun, changed a thoroughly-explored love affair into a one night stand. Oh, there was no question about it, this girl and I were finished, right this minute, as of now, because she was just as psychic as I was this morning and had sensed every last thing that I'd been thinking.

With a movement smooth enough not to look rushed I swung into a crouch. She was on her knees faster than that, her left hand hovering over the little set of tools for her stump, which like any good mechanic she'd lined up neatly on the edge of the blanket—the hook, the comb, a long telescoping fork, a couple of other items, and the knife. I'd grabbed a handful of blanket, ready to jerk it from under her. She'd seen that I'd grabbed it. Our gazes dueled.

There was a high-pitched whine over our heads! Quite loud from the start, though it sounded as if it were very deep up in the haze. It swiftly dropped in pitch and volume.

The top of the skeletal cracking plant across the freeway glowed with St. Elmo's fire! Three times it glowed that way, so bright we could see the violet-blue flames of it reaching up despite the full amber daylight.

The whine died away but in the last moment, paradoxically, it seemed to be coming closer!

This shared threat—for any unexpected event is a threat in the Deathlands and a mysterious event doubly so—put a stop to our murder game. The girl and I were buddies again, buddies to be relied on in a pinch, for the duration of the threat at least. No need to say so or to reassure each other of the fact in any way, it was taken for granted. Besides, there was no time. We had to use every second allowed us in getting ready for whatever was coming.

First I grabbed up Mother. Then I relieved myself—fear made it easy. Then I skinned into my pants and boots, slapped in my teeth, thrust the blanket and knapsack into the shallow cave under the edge of the freeway, looking around me all the time so as not to be surprised from any quarter.

Meanwhile the girl had put on her boots, located her dart gun, unscrewed the pliers from her stump, put the knife in, and was arranging her scarf so it made a sling for the maimed arm—I wondered why but had no time to waste guessing, even if I'd wanted to, for at that moment a small dull silver plane, beetle-shaped more than anything else, loomed out of the haze beyond the cracking plant and came silently drifting down toward us.

The girl thrust her satchel into the cave and along with it her dart gun. I caught her idea and tucked Mother into my pants behind my back.

I'd thought from the first glimpse of it that the plane was disabled—I guess it was its silence that gave me the idea. This theory was confirmed when one of its very stubby wings or vanes touched a corner pillar of the cracking plant. The plane was moving in too slow a glide to be wrecked, in fact it was moving in a slower glide than I would have believed possible—but then it's many years since I have seen a plane in flight.

It wasn't wrecked but the little collision spun it around twice in a lazy circle and it landed on the freeway with a scuffing noise not fifty feet from us. You couldn't exactly say it had crashed in, but it stayed at an odd tilt. It looked crippled all right.

An oval door in the plane opened and a man dropped lightly out on the concrete. And what a man! He was nearer seven feet tall than six, close-cropped blond hair, face and hands richly tanned, the rest of him covered by trim garments of a gleaming gray. He must have weighed as much as the two of us together, but he was beautifully built, muscular yet supple-seeming. His face looked brightly intelligent and even-tempered and kind.

Yes, kind!—damn him! It wasn't enough that his body should fairly glow with a health and vitality that was an insult to our seared skins and stringy muscles and ulcers and half-rotted stomachs and half-arrested cancers, he had to look kind too—the sort of man who would put you to bed and take care of you, as if you were some sort of interesting sick fox, and maybe even say a little prayer for you, and all manner of other abominations.

Idon't think I could have endured my fury standing still. Fortunately there was no need to. As if we'd rehearsed the whole thing for hours, the girl and I scrambled up onto the freeway and scurried toward the man from the plane, cunningly swinging away from each other so that it would be harder for him to watch the two of us at once, but not enough to make it obvious that we attended an attack from two quarters.

We didn't run though we covered the ground as fast as we dared—running would have been too much of a give-away too, and the Pilot, which was how I named him to myself, had a strange-looking small gun in his right hand. In fact the way we moved was part of our act—I dragged one leg as if it were crippled and the girl faked another sort of limp, one that made her approach a series of half curtsies. Her arm in the sling was all twisted, but at the same time she was accidently showing her breasts—I remember thinking *you won't distract this breed bull that way, sister, he probably has a harem of six-foot heifers.* I had my head thrown back and my hands stretched out supplicatingly. Meanwhile the both of us were babbling a blue streak. I was rapidly croaking something like, "Mister for God's sake save my pal he's hurt a lot worse'n I am not a hundred yards away he's dyin' mister he's dyin' o' thirst his tongue's black'n all swole up oh save him mister save my pal he's not a hundred yards away he's dyin' mister dyin'—" and she was singsonging an even worse rigamarole about how "they" were after us from Porter and going to crucify us because we believed in science and how they'd already impaled her mother and her ten-year-old sister and a lot more of the same.

It didn't matter that our stories didn't fit or make sense, the babble had a convincing tone and getting us closer to this guy, which was all that counted. He pointed his gun at me and then I could see him hesitate and I thought exultingly *it's a lot of healthy meat you got there, mister, but it's tame meat, mister, tame!*

He compromised by taking a step back and sort of hooting at us and waving us off with his left hand, as if we were a couple of stray dogs.

It was greatly to our advantage that we'd acted without hesitation, and I don't think we'd have been able to do that except that we'd been all set to kill each other when he dropped in. Our muscles and nerves and minds were keyed for instant ruthless attack. And some "civilized" people still say that the urge to murder doesn't contribute to self-preservation!

We were almost close enough now and he was steeling himself to shoot and I remember wondering for a split second what his damn gun did to you, and then me and the girl had started the alternation routine. I'd stop dead, as if completely cowed by the threat of his weapon, and as he took note of it she'd go in a little further, and as his gaze shifted to her she'd stop dead and I'd go in another foot and then try to make my halt even more convincing as his gaze darted back to me. We worked it perfectly, our rhythm was beautiful, as if we were old dancing partners, though the whole thing was absolutely impromptu.

Still, I honestly don't think we'd ever have got to him if it hadn't been for the distraction that came just then to help us. I could tell, you see, that he'd finally steeled himself and we still weren't quite close enough. He wasn't as tame as I'd hoped. I reached behind me for Mother, determined to do a last-minute rush and leap anyway, when there came this sick scream.

I don't know how else to describe it briefly. It was a scream, feminine for choice, it came from some distance and the direction of the old cracking plant, it had a note of anguish and warning, yet at the same time it was weak and almost faltering you might say and squeaky at the end, as if it came from a person half dead and a throat choked with phlegm. It had all those qualities or a wonderful mimicking of them.

And it had quite an effect on our boy in gray for in the act of shooting me down he started to turn and look over his shoulder.

Oh, it didn't altogether stop him from shooting me. He got me partly covered again as I was in the middle of my lunge. I found out what his gun did to you. My right arm, which was the part he'd covered, just went dead and I finished my lunge slamming up against his iron knees, like a highschool kid trying to block out a pro footballer, with the knife slipping uselessly away from my fingers.

But in the blessed meanwhile the girl had lunged too, not with a slow slash, thank God, but with a high, slicing thrust aimed arrow-straight for a point just under his ear.

She connected and a fan of blood sprayed her full in the face.

I grabbed my knife with my left hand as it fell, scrambled to my feet, and drove the knife at his throat in a round-house swing that happened to come handiest at the time. The point went through his flesh like nothing and jarred against his spine with a violence that I hoped would shock into nervous insensibility the stoutest medulla oblongata and prevent any dying reprisals on his part.

I got my wish, in large part. He swayed, straightened, dropped his gun, and fell flat on his back, giving his skull a murderous crack on the concrete for good measure. He lay there and after a half dozen gushes the bright blood quit pumping strongly out of his neck.

Then came the part that was like a dying reprisal, though obviously not being directed by him as of now. And come to think of it, it may have had its good points.

The girl, who was clearly a most cool-headed cuss, snatched for his gun where he'd dropped it, to make sure she got it ahead of me. She snatched, yes—and then jerked back, letting off a sizable squeal of pain, anger, and surprise.

Where we'd seen his gun hit the concrete there was now a tiny incandescent puddle. A rill of blood snaked out from the pool around his head and touched the whitely glowing puddle and a jet of steam sizzled up.

Somehow the gun had managed to melt itself in the moment of its owner dying. Well, at any rate that showed it hadn't contained any gunpowder or ordinary chemical explosives, though I already knew it operated on other principles from the way it had been used to paralyze me. More to the point, it showed that the gun's owner was the member of a culture that believed in taking very complete precautions against its gadgets falling into the hands of strangers.

But the gun fusing wasn't quite all. As the girl and me shifted our gaze from the puddle, which was cooling fast and now glowed red like the blood—as we shifted our gaze back from the puddle to the dead man, we saw that at three points (points over where you'd expect pockets to be) his gray clothing had charred in small irregularly shaped patches from which threads of black smoke were twisting upward.

Just at that moment, so close as to make me jump in spite of years of learning to absorb shocks stoically—right at my elbow it seemed to (the girl jumped too, I may say)—a voice said, "Done a murder, hey?"

Advancing briskly around the skewily grounded plane from the direction of the cracking plant was an old geezer, a seasoned, hard-baked Deathlander if I ever saw one. He had a shock of bone-white hair, the rest of him that showed from his weathered gray clothing looked fried by the sun's rays and others to a stringy crisp, and strapped to his boots and weighing down his belt were a good dozen knives.

Not satisfied with the unnerving noise he'd made already, he went on brightly, "Neat job too, I give you credit for that, but why the hell did you have to set the guy afire?"

CHAPTER THREE

We are always, thanks to our human nature, potential criminals. None of us stands outside humanity's black collective shadow.
—The Undiscovered Self,
by Carl Jung

Ordinarily scroungers who hide around on the outskirts until the killing's done and then come in to share the loot get what they deserve—wordless orders, well backed up, to be on their way at once. Sometimes they even catch an after-clap of the murder urge, if it hasn't all been expended on the first victim or victims. Yet they *will* do it, trusting I suppose to the irresistible glamor of their personalities. There were several reasons why we didn't at once give Pop this treatment.

In the first place we didn't neither of us have our distance weapons. My revolver and her dart gun were both tucked in the cave back at the edge of the freeway. And there's one bad thing about a bugger so knife-happy he lugs them around by the carload—he's generally good at tossing them. With his dozen or so knives Pop definitely outgunned us.

Second, we were both of us without the use of an arm. That's right, the both of us. My right arm still dangled like a string of sausages and I couldn't yet feel any signs of it coming undead. While she'd burned her fingers badly grabbing at the gun—I could see their red-splotched tips now as she pulled them out of her mouth for a second to wipe the Pilot's blood out of her eyes. All she had was her stump with the knife screwed to it. Me, I can throw a knife left-handed if I have to, but you bet I wasn't going to risk Mother that way.

Then I'd no sooner heard Pop's voice, breathy and a little high like an old man's will get, than it occurred to me that he must have been the one who had given the funny scream that had distracted the Pilot's attention and let us get him. Which incidentally made Pop a quick thinker and imaginative to boot, and meant that he'd helped on the killing.

Besides all that, Pop did not come in fawning and full of extravagant praise, as most scroungers will. He just assumed equality with us right from the start and he talked in an absolutely matter-of-fact way, neither praising nor criticizing one bit—too damn matter-of-fact and open, for that matter, to suit my taste, but then I have heard other buggers say that some old men are apt to get talkative, though I had never worked with or run into one myself. Old people are very rare in the Deathlands, as you might imagine.

So the girl and me just scowled at him but did nothing to stop him as he came along. Near us, his extra knives would be no advantage to him.

"Hum," he said, "looks a lot like a guy I murdered five years back down Los Alamos way. Same silver monkey suit and almost as tall. Nice chap too—was trying to give me something for a fever I'd faked. That his gun melted? My man didn't smoke after I gave him his quietus, but then it turned out he didn't have any metal on him. I wonder if this chap—" He started to kneel down by the body.

"Hands off, Pop!" I gritted at him. That was how we started calling him Pop.

"Why sure, sure," he said, staying there on one knee. "I won't lay a finger on him. It's just that I've heard the Alamosers have it rigged so that any metal they're carrying melts when they die, and I was wondering about this boy. But he's all yours, friend. By the way, what's your name, friend?"

"Ray," I snarled. "Ray Baker." I think the main reason I told him was that I didn't want him calling me "friend" again. "You talk too much, Pop."

"I suppose I do, Ray," he agreed. "What's your name, lady?"

The girl just sort of hissed at him and he grinned at me as if to say, "Oh, women!" Then he said, "Why don't you go through his pockets, Ray? I'm real curious."

"Shut up," I said, but I felt that he'd put me on the spot just the same. I was curious about the guy's pockets myself, of course, but I was also wondering if Pop was alone or if he had somebody with him, and whether there was anybody else in the plane or not—things like that, too many things. At the same time I didn't want to let on to Pop how useless my right arm was—if I'd just get a twinge of feeling in that arm, I knew I'd feel a lot more confident fast. I knelt down across the body from him, started to lay Mother aside and then hesitated.

The girl gave me an encouraging look, as if to say, "I'll take care of the old geezer." On the strength of her look I put down Mother and started to pry open the Pilot's left hand, which was clenched in a fist that looked a mite too big to have nothing inside it.

The girl started to edge behind Pop, but he caught the movement right away and looked at her with a grin that was so knowing and yet so friendly, and yet so pitying at the same time—with the pity of the old pro for even the seasoned amateur—that in her place I think I'd have blushed myself, as she did now...through the streaks of the Pilot's blood.

"You don't have to worry none about me, lady," he said, running a hand through his white hair and incidentally touching the pommel of one of the two knives strapped high on the back of his jacket so he could reach one over either shoulder. "I quit murdering some years back. It got to be too much of a strain on my nerves."

"Oh yeah?" I couldn't help saying as I pried up the Pilot's index finger and started on the next. "Then why the stab-factory, Pop?"

"Oh you mean those," he said, glancing down at his knives. "Well, the fact is, Ray, I carry them to impress buggers dumber than you and the lady here. Anybody wants to think I'm still a practicing murderer I got no objections. Matter of sentiment, too, I just hate to part with them—they bring back important memories. And then—you won't believe this, Ray, but I'm going to tell you just the same— guys just up and give me their knives and I doubly hate to part with a gift."

I wasn't going to say "Oh yeah?" again or "Shut up!" either, though I certainly wished I could turn off Pop's spigot, or thought I did. Then I felt a painful tingling shoot down my right arm. I smiled at Pop and said, "Any other reasons?"

"Yep," he said. "Got to shave and I might as well do it in style. A new blade every day in the fortnight is twice as good as the old ads. You know, it makes you keep a knife in fine shape if you shave with it. What you got there, Ray?"

"You were wrong, Pop," I said. "He did have some metal on him that didn't melt."

I held up for them to see the object I'd extracted from his left fist: a bright steel cube measuring about an inch across each side, but it felt lighter than if it were solid metal. Five of the faces looked absolutely bare. The sixth had a round button recessed in it.

From the way they looked at it neither Pop nor the girl had the faintest idea of what it was. I certainly hadn't.

"Had he pushed the button?" the girl asked. Her voice was throaty but unexpectedly refined, as if she'd done no talking at all, not even to herself, since coming to the

Deathlands and so retained the cultured intonations she'd had earlier, whenever and wherever that had been. It gave me a funny feeling, of course, because they were the first words I'd heard her speak.

"Not from the way he was holding it," I told her. "The button was pointed up toward his thumb but the thumb was on the outside of his fingers." I felt an unexpected satisfaction at having expressed myself so clearly and I told myself not to get childish.

The girl slitted her eyes. "Don't you push it, Ray," she said.

"Think I'm nuts?" I told her, meanwhile sliding the cube into the smaller pocket of my pants, where it fit tight and wouldn't turn sideways and the button maybe get pressed by accident. The tingling in my right arm was almost unbearable now, but I was getting control over the muscles again.

"Pushing that button," I added, "might melt what's left of the plane, or blow us all up." It never hurts to emphasize that you may have another weapon in your possession, even if it's just a suicide bomb.

"There was a man pushed another button once," Pop said softly and reflectively. His gaze went far out over the Deathlands and took in a good half of the horizon and he slowly shook his head. Then his face brightened. "Did you know, Ray," he said, "that I actually met that man? Long afterwards. You don't believe me, I know, but I actually did. Tell you about it some other time."

I almost said, "Thanks, Pop, for sparing me at least for a while," but I was afraid that would set him off again. Besides, it wouldn't have been quite true. I've heard other buggers tell the yarn of how they met (and invariably rubbed out) the actual guy who pushed the button or buttons that set the fusion missiles blasting toward their targets, but I felt a sudden curiosity as to what Pop's version of the yarn would be. Oh well, I could ask him some other time, if we both lived that long. I started to check the Pilot's pockets. My right hand could help a little now.

"Those look like mean burns you got there, lady," I heard Pop tell the girl. He was right. There were blisters easy to see on three of the fingertips. "I've got some salve that's pretty good," he went on, "and some clean cloth. I could put on a bandage for you if you wanted. If your hand started to feel poisoned you could always tell Ray here to slip a knife in me."

Pop was a cute gasser, you had to admit. I reminded myself that it was Pop's business to play up to the both of us, charm being the secret weapon of all scroungers.

The girl gave a harsh little laugh. "Very well," she said, "but we will use my salve, I know it works for me." And she started to lead Pop to where we'd hidden our things.

"I'll go with you," I told them, standing up.

It didn't look like we were going to have any more murders today—Pop had got through the preliminary ingratiations pretty well and the girl and me had had our catharsis—but that would be no excuse for any such stupidity as letting the two of them get near my .38.

Strolling to the cave and back I eased the situation a bit more by saying, "That scream you let off, Pop, really helped. I don't know what gave you the idea, but thanks."

"Oh that," he said. "Forget about it."

"I won't," I told him. "You may say you've quit killing, but helped on a do-in today."

"Ray," he said a little solemnly, "if it'll make you feel any happier, I'll take a bit of the responsibility for every murder that's been done since the beginning of time."

I looked at him for a while. Then, "Pop, you're not by any chance the religious type?" I asked suddenly.

"Lord, no," he told us.

That struck me as a satisfactory answer. God preserve me from the religious type! We have quite a few of those in the Deathlands. It generally means that they try to convert you to something before they kill you. Or sometimes afterwards.

We completed our errands. I felt a lot more secure with Old Financier's Friend strapped to my middle. Mother is wonderful but she is not enough.

I dawdled over inspecting the Pilot's pockets, partly to give my right hand time to come back all the way. And to tell the truth I didn't much enjoy the job—a corpse, especially such a handsome cadaver as this, just didn't go with Pop's brand of light patter.

Pop did up the girl's hand in high style, bandaging each finger separately and then persuading her to put on a big left-hand work glove he took out of his small pack.

"Lost the right," he explained, "which was the only one I ever used anyway. Never knew until now why I kept this. How does it feel, Alice?"

I might have known he'd worm her name out of her. It occurred to me that Pop's ideas of scrounging might extend to Alice's favors. The urge doesn't die out when you get old, they tell me. Not completely.

He'd also helped her replace the knife on her stump with the hook.

By that time I'd poked into all the Pilot's pockets I could get at without stripping him and found nothing but three irregularly shaped blobs of metal, still hot to the touch. Under the charred spots, of course.

I didn't want the job of stripping him. Somebody else could do a little work, I told myself. I've been bothered by bodies before (as who hasn't, I suppose?) but this one was really beginning to make me sick. Maybe I was cracking up, it occurred to me. Murder is a very wearing business, as all

Deathlanders know, and although some crack earlier than others, all crack in the end.

I must have been showing how I was feeling because, "Cheer up, Ray," Pop said. "You and Alice have done a big murder—I'd say the subject was six foot ten—so you ought to be happy. You've drawn a blank on his pockets but there's still the plane."

"Yeah, that's right," I said, brightening a little. "There's still the stuff in the plane." I knew there were some items I couldn't hope for, like .38 shells, but there'd be food and other things.

"Nuh-uh," Pop corrected me. "I said *the plane*. You may have thought it's wrecked, but I don't. Have you taken a real gander at it? It's worth doing, believe me."

I jumped up. My heart was suddenly pounding. I was glad of an excuse to get away from the body, but there was a lot more in my feelings than that. I was filled with an excitement to which I didn't want to give a name because it would make the let-down too great.

One of the wide stubby wings of the plane, raking downward so that its tip almost touched the concrete, had hidden the undercarriage of the fuselage from our view. Now, coming around the wing, I saw that *there was no undercarriage.*

I had to drop to my hands and knees and scan around with my cheek next to the concrete before I'd believe it. *The "wrecked" plane was at all points at least six inches off the ground.*

I got to my feet again. I was shaking. I wanted to talk but I couldn't. I grabbed the leading edge of the wing to stop from falling. The whole body of the plane gave a fraction of an inch and then resisted my leaning weight with lazy power, just like a gyroscope.

"Antigravity," I croaked, though you couldn't have heard me two feet. Then my voice came back. "Pop, Alice! They got antigravity! Antigravity—and it's working!"

Alice had just come around the wing and was facing me. She was shaking too and her face was white like I knew mine was. Pop was politely standing off a little to one side, watching us curiously. "Told you you'd won a real prize," he said in his matter-of-fact way.

Alice wet her lips. "Ray," she said, "we can get away."

Just those four words, but they did it. Something in me unlocked—no, exploded describes it better.

"We can go places!" I almost shouted.

"Beyond the dust," she said. "Mexico City. South America!" She was forgetting the Deathlander's cynical article of belief that the dust never ends, but then so was I. It makes a difference whether or not you've got a means of doing something.

"Rio!" I topped her with. "The Indies. Hong Kong. Bombay. Egypt. Bermuda. The French Riviera!"

"Bullfights and clean beds," she burst out with. "Restaurants. Swimming pools. Bathrooms!"

"Skindiving," I took it up with, as hysterical as she was. "Road races and roulette tables."

"Bentleys and Porsches!"

"Aircoups and DC4s and Comets!"

"Martinis and hashish and ice cream sodas!"

"Hot food! Fresh coffee! Gambling, smoking, dancing, music, drinks!" I was going to add *women*, but then I thought of how hard-bitten little Alice would look beside the dream creatures I had in mind. I tactfully suppressed the word but I filed the idea away.

I don't think either of us knew exactly what we were saying. Alice in particular I don't believe was old enough to have experienced almost any of the things the words referred to. They were mysterious symbols of long-interdicted delights spewing out of us.

"Ray," Alice said, hurrying to me, "let's get aboard."

"Yes," I said eagerly and then I saw a little problem. The door to the plane was a couple of feet above our heads. Whoever hoisted himself up first—or got hoisted up, as would have to be the case with Alice on account of her hand—would be momentarily at the other's mercy. I guess it occurred to Alice too because she stopped and looked at me. It was a little like the old teaser about the fox, the goose, and the corn.

Maybe, too, we were both a little scared the plane was booby-trapped.

Pop solved the problem in the direct way I might have expected of him by stepping quietly between us, giving a light leap, catching hold of the curving sill, chinning himself on it, and scrambling up into the plane so quickly that we'd hardly have had time to do anything about it if we'd wanted to. Pop couldn't be much more than a bantamweight, even with all his knives. The plane sagged an inch and then swung up again.

As Pop disappeared from view I backed off, reaching for my .38, but a moment later he stuck out his head and grinned down at us, resting his elbows on the sill.

"Come on up," he said. "It's quite a place. I promise not to push any buttons 'til you get here, though there's whole regiments of them."

I grinned back at Pop and gave Alice a boost up. She didn't like it, but she could see it had to be her next. She hooked onto the sill and Pop caught hold of her left wrist below the big glove and heaved.

Then it was my turn. I didn't like it. I didn't like the idea of those two buggers poised above me while my hands were helpless on the sill. But I thought *Pop's a nut. You can trust a nut, at least a little ways, though you can't trust nobody else.* I heaved myself up. It was strange to feel the plane giving and then bracing itself like something alive. It seemed to have no trouble accepting our combined weight, which after all was hardly more than half again the Pilot's.

Inside the cabin was pretty small but as Pop had implied, oh my! Everything looked soft and smoothly curved, like you imagine your insides being, and almost everything was a restfully dull silver. The general shape of it was something like the inside of an egg. Forward, which was the larger end, were a couple of screens and a wide viewport and some small dials and the button brigades Pop had mentioned, lined up like blank typewriter keys but enough for writing Chinese.

Just aft of the instrument panel were two very comfortable-looking strange low seats. They seemed to be facing backwards until I realized they were meant to be knelt into. The occupant, I could see, would sort of sprawl forward, his hands free for button-pushing and such. There were spongy chinrests.

Aft was a tiny instrument panel and a kind of sideways seat, not nearly so fancy. The door by which we'd entered was to the side, a little aft.

I didn't see any indications of cabinets or fixed storage spaces of any kinds, but somehow stuck to the walls here and there were quite a few smooth blobby packages, mostly dull silver too, some large, some small—valises and handbags, you might say.

All in all, it was a lovely cabin and, more than that, it seemed lived in. It looked as if it had been shaped for, and maybe by one man. It had a personality you could feel, a strong but warm personality of its own.

Then I realized whose personality it was. I almost got sick—so close to it I started telling myself it must be something antigravity did to your stomach.

But it was all too interesting to let you get sick right away. Pop was poking into two of the large mound-shaped cases that were sitting loose and open on the right-hand seat, as if ready for emergency use. One had a folded something with straps on it that was probably a parachute. The second had I judged a thousand or more of the inch cubes such as I'd pried out of the Pilot's hand, all neatly stacked in a cubical box inside the soft outer bag. You could see the one-cube gap where he'd taken the one.

I decided to take the rest of the bags off the walls and open them, if I could figure out how. The others had the same idea, but Alice had to take off her hook and put on her pliers, before she could make progress. Pop helped her. There was room enough for us to do these things without crowding each other too closely.

By the time Alice was set to go I'd discovered the trick of getting the bags off. You couldn't pull them away from the wall no matter what force you used, at least I couldn't, and you couldn't even slide them straight along the walls, but if you just gave them a gentle counterclockwise twist they came off like nothing. Twisting them clockwise glued them back on. It was very strange, but I told myself that if these boys could generate antigravity fields they could create screwy fields of other sorts.

It also occurred to me to wonder if "these boys" came from Earth. The Pilot had looked human enough, but these accomplishments didn't—not by my standards for human achievement in the Age of the Deaders. At any rate I had to admit to myself that my pet term "cultural queer" did not describe to my own satisfaction members of a culture which could create things like this cabin. Not that I liked making the admission. It's hard to admit an exception to a pet gripe against things.

The excitement of getting down and opening the Christmas packages saved me from speculating too much along these or any other lines.

I hit a minor jackpot right away. In the same bag were a compass, a catalytic pocket lighter, a knife with a saw-tooth back edge that made my affection for Mother waver, a dust mask, what looked like a compact water-filtration unit, and several other items adding up to a deluxe Deathlands Survival Kit.

There were some goggles in the kit I didn't savvy until I put them on and surveyed the landscape out the viewport. A nearby dust drift I knew to be hot glowed green as death in the slightly smoky lenses. Wow! Those specs had Geiger counters beat a mile and I privately bet myself they worked at night. I stuck them in my pocket quick.

We found bunches of tiny electronics parts—I think they were; spools of magnetic tape, but nothing to play it on; reels of very narrow film with frames much too small to see anything at all unmagnified; about three thousand cigarettes in unlabeled transparent packs of twenty—we lit up quick, using my new lighter; a picture book that didn't make much sense because the views might have been of tissue sections or starfields, we couldn't quite decide, and there were no captions to help; a thin book with ricepaper pages covered with Chinese characters—*that* was a puzzler; a thick book with nothing but columns of figures, all zeros and ones and nothing else; some tiny chisels; and a mouth organ. Pop, who'd make a point of just helping in the hunt, appropriated that last item—I might have known he would, I told myself. Now we could expect "Turkey in the Straw" at odd moments.

Alice found a whole bag of what were women's things judging from the frilliness of the garments included. She set aside some squeeze-packs and little gadgets and elastic items right away, but she didn't take any of the clothes. I caught her measuring some kind of transparent chemise against herself when she thought we weren't looking; it was for a girl maybe six sizes bigger.

And we found food. Cans of food that was heated up inside by the time you got the top rolled off, though the outside could still be cool to the touch. Cans of boneless steak, boneless chops, cream soup, peas, carrots, and fried potatoes—they weren't labeled at all but you could generally guess the contents from the shape of the can. Eggs that heated when you touched them and were soft-boiled evenly and barely firm by the time you had the shell broke. And small plastic bottles of strong coffee that heated up hospitably too—in this case the tops did a five-second hesitation in the middle of your unscrewing them.

At that point as you can imagine we let the rest of the packages go and had ourselves a feast. The food ate even better than it smelled. It was real hard for me not to gorge.

Then as I was slurping down my second bottle of coffee I happened to look out the viewport and see the Pilot's body and the darkening puddle around it and the coffee began to taste, well, not bad, but sickening. I don't think it was guilty conscience. Deathlanders outgrow those if they ever have them to start with; loners don't keep consciences—it takes cultures to give you those and make them work. Artistic inappropriateness is the closest I can come to describing what bothered me. Whatever it was, it made me feel lousy for a minute.

About the same time Alice did an odd thing with the last of *her* coffee. She slopped it on a rag and used it to wash her face. I guess she'd caught a reflection of herself with the blood smears. She didn't eat any more after that either. Pop kept on chomping away, a slow feeder and appreciative.

To be doing something I started to inspect the instrument panel and right away I was all excited again. The two screens were what got me. They showed shadowy maps, one of North America, the other of the World. The first one was a whole lot like the map I'd been imagining earlier—faint colors marked the small "civilized" areas including one in Eastern Canada and another in Upper Michigan that must be "countries" I didn't know about, and the Deathlands were real dark just as I'd always maintained they should be!

South of Lake Michigan was a brightly luminous green point that must be where we were, I decided. And for some reason the colored areas representing Los Alamos and Atlantic Highlands were glowing brighter than the others—they had an active luminosity. Los Alamos was blue, Atla-Hi violet. Los Alamos was shown having more territory than I expected. Savannah Fortress for that matter was a whole *lot* bigger than I'd have made it, pushing out pseudopods west and northeast along the coast, though its red didn't have the extra glow. But its growth-pattern reeked of imperialism.

The World screen showed dim color patches too, but for the moment I was more interested in the other.

The button armies marched right up to the lower edge of the screens and right away I got the crazy hunch that they were connected with spots on the map. Push the button for a certain spot and the plane would go there! Why, one button even seemed to have a faint violet nimbus around it (or else my eyes were going bad) as if to say, "Push me and we go to Atlantic Highlands."

A crazy notion as I say and no sensible way to handle a plane's navigation according to any standards I could imagine, but then as I've also said this plane didn't seem to be designed according to any standards but rather in line with one man's ideas, including his whims.

At any rate that was my hunch about the buttons and the screens. It tantalized rather than helped, for the only button that seemed to be marked in any way was the one (guessing by color) for Atlantic Highlands, and I certainly didn't want to go there. Like Alamos, Atla-Hi has the reputation for being a mysteriously dangerous place. Not openly mean and death-on-Deathlanders like Walla Walla or Porter, but buggers who swing too close to Atla-Hi have a way of never turning up again. You never expect to see again two out of three buggers who pass in the night, but for three out of three to keep disappearing is against statistics.

Alice was beside me now, scanning things over too, and from the way she frowned and what not I gathered she had caught my hunch and also shared my puzzlement.

Now was the time, all right, when we needed an instruction manual and not one in Chinese neither!

Pop swallowed a mouthful and said, "Yep, now'd be a good time to have him back for a minute, to explain things a bit. Oh, don't take offense, Ray, I know how it was for you and for you too, Alice. I know the both of you *had* to murder him, it wasn't a matter of free choice, it's the way us Deathlanders are built. Just the same, it'd be nice to have a way of killing 'em and keeping them on hand at the same time. I remember feeling that way after murdering the Alamoser I told you about. You see, I come down with the very fever I'd faked and almost died of it, while the man who could have cured me easy wouldn't do nothing but perfume the landscape with the help of a gang of anaerobic bacteria. Stubborn single-minded cuss!"

The first part of that oration started up my sickness again and irked me not a little. Dammit, what right had Pop to talk about how all us Deathlanders *had to* kill (which was true enough and by itself would have made me cotton to him) if as he'd claimed earlier *he'd* been able to quit killing? Pop was, an old hypocrite, I told myself—he'd helped murder the Pilot, he'd admitted as much—and Alice and me'd be better off if we bedded the both of them down together. But then the second part of what Pop said so made me want to feel pleasantly sorry for myself and laugh at the same time that I forgave the old geezer. Practically everything Pop said had that reassuring touch of insanity about it.

So it was Alice who said, "Shut up, Pop"—and rather casually at that—and she and me went on to speculate and then to argue about which buttons we ought to push, if any and in what order.

"Why not just start anywhere and keep pushing 'em one after another?—you're going to have to eventually, may as well start now," was Pop's light-hearted contribution to the discussion. "Got to take some chances in this life." He was sitting in the back seat and still nibbling away like a white-topped mangy old squirrel.

Of course Alice and me knew more than that. We kept making guesses as to how the buttons worked and then backing up our guesses with hot language. It was a little like two savages trying to decide how to play chess by looking at the pieces. And then the old escape-to-paradise theme took hold of us again and we studied the colored blobs on the World screen, trying to decide which would have the fanciest accommodations for blase ex-murderers. On the North America screen too there was an intriguing pink patch in southern Mexico that seemed to take in old Mexico City and Acapulco too.

"Quit talking and start pushing," Pop prodded us. "This way you're getting nowhere fast. I can't stand hesitation, it riles my nerves."

Alice thought you ought to push ten buttons at once, using both hands, and she was working out patterns for me to try. But I was off on a kick about how we should darken the plane to see if any of the other buttons glowed beside the one with the Atla-Hi violet.

"Look here, you killed a big man to get this plane," Pop broke in, coming up behind me. "Are you going to use it for discussion groups or are you going to fly it?"

"Quiet," I told him. I'd got a new hunch and was using the dark glasses to scan the instrument panel. They didn't show anything.

"Dammit, I can't stand this any more," Pop said and reached a hand and arm between us and brought it down on about fifty buttons, I'd judge.

The other buttons just went down and up, but the Atla-Hi button went down and stayed down.

The violet blob of Atla-Hi on the screen got even brighter in the next few moments.

The door closed with a tiny thud.

We took off.

CHAPTER FOUR

Any man who deals in murder, must have very incorrect ways of thinking, and truly inaccurate principles.
—Thomas de Quincey in
Murder Considered as One of the Fine Arts

For that matter we took off *fast* with the plane swinging to beat hell. Alice and me was in the two kneeling seats and we hugged them tight, but Pop was loose and sort of rattled around the cabin for a while—and serve him right!

On one of the swings I caught a glimpse of the seven dented gas tanks, looking like dull crescents from this angle through the orange haze and getting rapidly smaller as they hazed out.

After a while the plane levelled off and quit swinging, and a while after that my image of the cabin quit swinging too. Once again I just managed to stave off the vomits, this time the vomits from natural causes. Alice looked very pale around the gills and kept her face buried in the chinrest of her chair.

Pop ended up right in our faces, sort of spread-eagled against the instrument panel. In getting himself off it he must have braced his hands against half the buttons at one time or another and I noticed that none of them went down a fraction. They were *locked*. It had probably happened automatically when the Atla-Hi button got pushed.

I'd have stopped him messing around in that apish way, but with the ultra-queasy state of my stomach I lacked all ambition and was happy just not to be smelling him so close.

I still wasn't taking too great an interest in things as I idly watched the old geezer rummaging around the cabin for something that got misplaced in the shake-up. Eventually he found it—a small almond-shaped can. He opened it. Sure enough it turned out to have almonds in it. He fitted himself in the back seat and munched them one at a time. Ish!

"Nothing like a few nuts to top off with," he said cheerfully.

I could have cut his throat even more cheerfully, but the damage had been done and you think twice before you kill a person in close quarters when you aren't absolutely sure you'll be able to dispose of the body. How did I know I'd be able to open the door? I remember philosophizing that Pop ought at least to have broke an arm so he'd be as badly off as Alice and me (though for that matter my right arm was fully recovered now) but he was all in one piece. There's no justice in events, that's for sure.

The plane ploughed along silently through the orange soup, though there was really no way to tell it was moving now—until a skewy spindle shape loomed up ahead and shot back over the viewport. I think it was a vulture. I don't know how vultures manage to operate in the haze, which ought to cancel their keen eyesight, but they do. It shot past *fast*.

Alice lifted her face out of the sponge stuff and began to study the buttons again. I heaved myself up and around a little and said, "Pop, Alice and me are going to try to work out how this plane navigates. This time we don't want no interference." I didn't say a word more about what he'd done. It never does to hash over stupidities.

"That's perfectly fine, go right ahead," he told me. "I feel calm as a kitten now we're going somewheres. That's all that ever matters with me." He chuckled a bit and added, "You got to admit I gave you and Alice something to work with," but then he had the sense to shut up tight.

We weren't so chary of pushing buttons this time, but ten minutes or so convinced us that you couldn't push any of the buttons any more, they *were* all locked down—all locked except for maybe one, which we didn't try at first for a special reason.

We looked for other controls—sticks, levers, pedals, finger-holes and the like. There weren't any. Alice went back and tried the buttons on Pop's minor console. They were locked too. Pop looked interested but didn't say a word.

We realized in a general way what had happened, of course. Pushing the Atla-Hi button had set us on some kind of irreversible automatic. I couldn't imagine the why of gimmicking a plane's controls like that, unless maybe to keep loose children or prisoners from being able to mess things up while the pilot took a snooze, but there were a lot of whys to this plane that didn't seem to have any standard answers.

The business of taking off on irreversible automatic had happened so neatly that I naturally wondered whether Pop might not know more about navigating this plane than he let on, a whole lot more in fact, and the seemingly idiotic petulance of his pushing all the buttons have been a shrewd cover for pushing the Atla-Hi button. But if Pop had been acting he'd been acting beautifully, with a serene disregard for the chances of breaking his own neck. I decided this was a possibility I could think about later and maybe act on then, after Alice and me had worked through the more obvious stuff.

The reason we hadn't tried the one button yet was that it showed a green nimbus, just like the Atla-Hi button had had a violet nimbus. Now there was no green on either of the screens except for the tiny green star that I had figured stood for the plane and it didn't make sense to go where we already were. And if it meant some other place, some place not shown on the screens, you bet we weren't going to be too quick about deciding to go there. It might not be on Earth.

Alice expressed it by saying, "My namesake was always a little too quick at responding to those DRINK ME cues."

I suppose she thought she was being cryptic, but I fooled her. "*Alice in Wonderland?*" I asked. She nodded, and gave me a little smile, not at all like one of the EAT ME smiles she'd given me last evening.

It is funny how crazily happy a little touch of the intellectual past like that can make you feel—and how horribly uncomfortable a moment later.

We both started to study the North America screen again and almost at once we realized that it had changed in one small particular. The green star had twinned. Where there had been one point of green light there were now two, very close together like the double star in the handle of the Dipper. We watched it for a while. The distance between the two stars grew perceptibly greater. We watched it for a while longer, considerably longer. It became clear that the position of the more westerly star on the screen was fixed, while the more easterly star was moving east toward Atla-Hi with about the speed of the tip of the minute hand on a wrist watch (two inches an hour, say). The pattern began to make sense.

I figured it this way: the moving star must stand for the plane, the other green dot must stand for where the plane had just been. For some reason the spot on the freeway by the old cracking plant was recognized as a marked locality by the screen. Why I don't know. It reminded me of the old "X Marks the Spot" of newspaper murders, but that would be getting very fancy. Anyway the spot we'd just taken off from was so marked and in that case the button with the green nimbus...

"Hold tight, everybody," I said to Alice, grudgingly including Pop in my warning. "I got to try it."

I gripped my seat with my knees and one arm and pushed the green button. It pushed.

The plane swung around in a level loop, not too tight to disturb the stomach much, and steadied out again.

I couldn't judge how far we'd swung but Alice and me watched the green stars and after about a minute she said, "They're getting closer," and a little while later I said, "Yeah, for sure."

I scanned the board. The green button—the cracking-plant button, to call it that—was locked down of course. The Atla-Hi button was up, glowing violet. All the other buttons were still up and *locked* up—I tried them all again.

It was clear as day used to be. We could either go to Atla-Hi or we could go back where we'd started from. There was no third possibility.

It was a little hard to take. You think of a plane as freedom, as something that will carry you anywhere in the world you choose to go, especially any paradise, and then you find yourself worse limited than if you'd stayed on the ground—at least that was the way it was happening to us.

But Alice and me were realists. We knew it wouldn't help to wail. We were up against another of those "two" problems, the problem of two destinations, and we had to choose ours.

If we go back, I thought, *we can trek on somewhere—anywhere—richer by the loot from the plane, especially that Survival Kit. Trek on with some loot we'll mostly never understand and with the knowledge that we are leaving a plane that can fly, that we are shrinking back from an unknown adventure.*

Also if we go back there's something else we'll have to face, something we'll have to live with for a little while at least that won't be nice to live with after this cozily personal cabin, something that shouldn't bother me at all but, dammit, it does.

Alice made the decision for us and at the same time showed she was thinking about the same thing as me.

"I don't want to have to smell him, Ray," she said. "I am not going back to keep company with that filthy corpse. I'd rather anything than that." And she pushed the Atla-Hi button again and as the plane started to swing she looked at me defiantly as if to say I'd reverse the course again over her dead body.

"Don't tense up," I told her. "I want a new shake of the dice myself."

"You know, Alice," Pop said reflectively, "it was the smell of my Alamoser got to me too. I just couldn't bear it. I couldn't get away from it because my fever had me pinned down, so there was nothing left for me to do but go crazy. No Atla-Hi for me, just Bug-land. My mind died, though not my memory. By the time I'd got my strength back I'd started to be a new bugger. I didn't know no more about living than a newborn babe, except I knew I couldn't go back—go back to murdering and all that. My new mind knew that much though otherwise it was just a blank. It was all very funny."

"And then I suppose," Alice cut in, her voice corrosive with sarcasm, "you hunted up a wandering preacher, or perhaps a kindly old hermit who lived on hot manna, and he showed you the blue sky!"

"Why no, Alice," Pop said. "I told you I don't go for religion. As it happens, I hunted me up a couple of murderers, guys who were worse cases then myself but who'd wanted to quit because it wasn't getting them nowhere and who'd found, I'd heard, a way of quitting, and the three of us had a long talk together."

"And they told you the great secret of how to live in the Deathlands without killing," Alice continued acidly. "Drop the nonsense, Pop. It can't be done."

"It's hard, I'll grant you," Pop said. "You have to go crazy or something almost as bad—in fact, maybe going crazy is the easiest way. But it can be done and, in the long run, murder is even harder."

I decided to interrupt this idle chatter. Since we were now definitely headed for Atla-Hi and there was nothing to do until we got there, unless one of us got a brainstorm about the controls, it was time to start on the less obvious stuff I'd tabled in my mind.

"Why are you on this plane, Pop?" I asked sharply. "What do you figure on getting out of Alice and me?—and I don't mean the free meals."

He grinned. His teeth were white and even—plates, of course. "Why, Ray," he said, "I was just giving Alice the reason. I like to talk to murderers, practicing murderers preferred. I need to—*have* to talk to 'em, to keep myself straight. Otherwise I might start killing again and I'm not up to that any more."

"Oh, so you get your kicks at second hand, you old peeper," Alice put in but, "Quit lying, Pop," I said. "About having quit killing, for one thing. In my books, which happen to be the old books in this case, the accomplice is every bit as guilty as the man with the slicer. You helped us kill the Pilot by giving that funny scream and you know it."

"Who says I did?" Pop countered, rearing up a little. "I never said so. I just said, 'Forget it.'" He hesitated a moment, studying me. Then he said, "I wasn't the one gave that scream. In fact, I'd have stopped it if I'd been able."

"Who did then?"

Again he studied me as he hesitated. "I'm not telling," he said, settling back.

"Pop!" I said, sharp again. "Buggers who pad together tell everything."

"Oh yeah," he agreed, smiling. "I remember saying that to quite a few guys in my day. It's a very restful comradely sentiment. I killed every last one of 'em, too."

"You may have, Pop," I granted, "but we're two to one."

"So you are," he agreed softly, looking the both of us over. I knew what he was thinking—that Alice still had just her pliers on and that in these close quarters his knives were as good as my gun.

"Give me your right hand, Alice," I said. Without taking my eyes off Pop I reached the knife without a handle out of her belt and then I started to unscrew the pliers out of her stump.

"Pop," I said as I did so, "you may have quit killing for all I know. I mean you may have quit killing clean decent Deathland style. But I don't believe one bit of that guff about having to talk to murderers to keep your mind sweet. Furthermore—"

"It's true though," he interrupted. "I got to keep myself reminded of how lousy it feels to be a murderer."

"So?" I said. "Well, here's one person who believes you've got a more practical reason for being on this plane. Pop, what's the bounty Atla-Hi gives you for every Deathlander you bring in? What would it be for two live Deathlanders? And what sort of reward would they pay for a lost plane brought in? Seems to me they might very well make you a citizen for that."

"Yes, even give you your own church," Alice added with a sort of wicked gaiety. I squeezed her stump gently to tell her let me handle it.

"Why, I guess you can believe that if you want to," Pop said and let out a soft breath. "Seems to me you need a lot of coincidences and happenstances to make that theory hold water, but you sure can believe it if you want to. I got no way, Ray, to prove to you I'm telling the truth except to say I am."

"Right," I said and then I threw the next one at him real fast. "What's more, Pop, weren't you traveling in this plane to begin with? That cuts a happenstance. Didn't you hop out while we were too busy with the Pilot to notice and just *pretend* to be coming from the cracking plant? Weren't the buttons locked because you were the Pilot's prisoner?"

Pop creased his brow thoughtfully. "It could have been that way," he said at last. "Could have been—according to the evidence as you saw it. It's quite a bright idea, Ray. I can almost see myself skulking in this cabin, while you and Alice—"

"You were skulking somewhere," I said. I finished screwing in the knife and gave Alice back her hand. "I'll repeat it, Pop," I said. "We're two to one. You'd better talk."

"Yes," Alice added, disregarding my previous hint. "You may have given up fighting, Pop, but I haven't. Not fighting, nor killing, nor anything in between those two. Any least thing." My girl was being her most pantherish.

"Now who says I've given up *fighting*?" Pop demanded, rearing a little again. "You people assume too much, it's a dangerous habit. Before we have any trouble and somebody squawks about me cheating, let's get one thing straight. If anybody jumps me I'll try to disable them, I'll try to hurt them in any way short of killing, and that means hamstringing and rabbit-punching and everything else. Every least thing, Alice. And if they happen to die while I'm honestly just trying to hurt them in a way short of killing, then I won't grieve too much. My conscience will be reasonably clear. Is that understood?"

I had to admit that it was. Pop might be lying about a lot of things, but I just didn't believe he was lying about this. And I already knew Pop was quick for his age and strong enough. If Alice and me jumped him now there'd be blood let six different ways. You can't jump a man who has a dozen knives easy to hand and not expect that to happen, two to one or not. We'd get him in the end but it would be gory.

"And now," Pop said quietly, "I *will* talk a little if you don't mind. Look here, Ray...Alice...the two of you are confirmed murderers, I know you wouldn't tell me nothing different, and being such you both know that there's nothing in murder in the long run. It satisfies a hunger and maybe gets you a little loot and it lets you get on to the next killing. But that's all, absolutely all. Yet you got to do it because it's the way you're built. The urge is there, it's an overpowering urge, and you got nothing to oppose it with. You feel the Big Grief and the Big Resentment, the dust is eating at your bones, you can't stand the city squares—the Porterites and Mantenors and such—because you know they're whistling in the dark and it's a dirty tune, so you go on killing. But if there were a decent practical way to quit, you'd take it. At least I think you would. When you still thought this plane could take you to Rio or Europe you felt that way, didn't you? You weren't planning to go there as murderers, were you? You were going to leave your trade behind."

It was pretty quiet in the cabin for a couple of seconds. Then Alice's thin laugh sliced the silence. "We were dreaming then," she said. "We were out of our heads. But now you're talking about practical things, as you say. What do you expect us to do if we quit our trade, as you call it—go into Walla Walla or Ouachita and give ourselves up? I might lose more than my right hand at Ouachita this time—that was just on suspicion."

"Or Atla-Hi," I added meaningfully. "Are you expecting us to admit we're murderers when we get to Atla-Hi, Pop?"

The old geezer smiled and thinned his eyes. "Now that wouldn't accomplish much, would it? Most places they'd just string you up, maybe after tickling your pain nerves a bit, or if it was Manteno they might put you in a cage and feed you slops and pray over you, and would that help you or anybody else? If a man or woman quits killing there's a lot of things he's got to straighten out—first his own mind and feelings, next he's got to do what he can to make up for the murders he's done—help the next of kin if any and so on—then he's got to carry the news to other killers who haven't heard it yet. He's got no time to waste being hanged. Believe me, he's got work lined up for him, work that's got to be done mostly in the Deathlands, and it's the sort of work the city squares can't help him with one bit, because they just don't understand us murderers and what makes us tick. We have to do it ourselves."

"Hey, Pop," I cut in, getting a little interested in the argument (there wasn't anything else to get interested in until we got to Atla-Hi or Pop let down his guard), "I dig you on the city squares (I call 'em cultural queers) and what sort of screwed-up fatheads they are, but just the same for a man to quit killing he's got to quit lone-wolfing it. He's got to belong to a community, he's got to have a culture of some sort, no matter how disgusting or nutsy."

"Well," Pop said, "don't us Deathlanders have a culture? With customs and folkways and all the rest? A very tight little culture, in fact. Nutsy as all get out, of course, but that's one of the beauties of it."

"Oh sure," I granted him, "but it's a culture based on murder and devoted wholly to murder. Murder is our way of life. That gets your argument nowhere, Pop."

"Correction," he said. "Or rather, re-interpretation." And now for a little while his voice got less old-man harsh and yet bigger somehow, as if it were more than just Pop talking. "Every culture," he said, "is a way of growth as well as a way of life, because the first law of life is growth. Our Deathland culture is devoted to growing *through* murder *away from* murder. That's my thought. It's about the toughest way of growth anybody was ever asked to face up to, but it's a way of growth just the same. A lot bigger and fancier cultures never could figure out the answer to the problem of war and killing—*we* know that, all right, we inhabit their grandest failure. Maybe us Deathlanders, working with murder every day, unable to pretend that it isn't part of every one of us, unable to put it out of our minds like the city squares do— maybe us Deathlanders are the ones to do that little job."

"But hell, Pop," I objected, getting excited in spite of myself, "even if we got a culture here in the Deathlands, a culture that can grow, it ain't a culture that can deal with repentant murderers. In a *real* culture a murderer feels guilty and confesses and then he gets hanged or imprisoned a long time and that squares things for him and everybody. You need religion and courts and hangmen and screws and all the rest of it. I don't think it's enough for a man just to say he's sorry and go around glad-handing other killers—*that* isn't going to be enough to wipe out his sense of guilt."

Pop squared his eyes at mine. "Are you so fancy that you have to have a sense of guilt, Ray?" he demanded. "Can't you just see when something's lousy? A sense of guilt's a luxury. Of course it's not enough to say you're sorry—you're going to have to spend a good part of the rest of your life making up for what you've done...and what you will do, too! But about hanging and prisons—was it ever proved those were the right thing for murderers? As for religion now—some of us who've quit killing are religious and a lot of us (me included) aren't; and some of the ones that are religious figure (maybe because there's no way for them to get hanged) that they're damned eternally—but that doesn't stop them doing good work. I ask you now, is any little thing like being damned eternally a satisfactory excuse for behaving like a complete rat?"

That did it, somehow. That last statement of Pop's appealed so much to me and was completely crazy at the same time, that I couldn't help warming up to him. Don't get me wrong, I didn't really fall for his line of chatter at all, but I found it fun to go along with it—so long as the plane was in this shuttle situation and we had nothing better to do.

Alice seemed to feel the same way. I guess any bugger that could kid religion the way Pop could got a little silver star in her books. Bronze, anyway.

Right away the atmosphere got easier. To start with we asked Pop to tell us about this "us" he kept mentioning and he said it was some dozens (or hundreds—nobody had accurate figures) of killers who'd quit and went nomading around the Deathlands trying to recruit others and help those who wanted to be helped. They had semi-permanent meeting places where they tried to get together at pre-arranged dates, but mostly they kept on the go, by twos and threes or—more rarely—alone. They were all men so far, at least Pop hadn't heard of any women members, but—he assured Alice earnestly—he would personally guarantee that there would be no objections to a girl joining up. They had recently taken to calling themselves Murderers Anonymous, after some pre-war organization Pop didn't know the original purpose of. Quite a few of them had slipped and gone back to murdering again, but some of these had come back after a while, more determined than ever to make a go of it.

"We welcomed 'em, of course," Pop said. "We welcome everybody. Everybody that's a genuine murderer, that is, and says he wants to quit. Guys that aren't blooded yet we draw the line at, no matter how fine they are."

Also, "We have a lot of fun at our meetings," Pop assured us. "You never saw such high times. Nobody's got a right to go glooming around or pull a long face just because he's done a killing or two. Religion or no religion, pride's a sin."

Alice and me ate it all up like we was a couple of kids and Pop was telling us fairy tales. That's what it all was, of course, a fairy tale—a crazy mixed-up fairy tale. Alice and me knew there could be no fellowship of Deathlanders like Pop was describing—it was impossible as blue sky—but it gave us a kick to pretend to ourselves for a while to believe in it.

Pop could talk forever, apparently, about murder and murderers and he had a bottomless bag of funny stories on the same topic and character vignettes—the murderers who were forever wanting their victims to understand and forgive them, the ones who thought of themselves as little kings with divine rights of dispensing death, the ones who insisted on laying down (chastely) beside their finished victims and playing dead for a couple of hours, the ones who weren't so chaste, the ones who could only do their killings when they were dressed a certain way (and the troubles they had with their murder costumes), the ones who could only kill people with certain traits or of a certain appearance (red-heads, say, or people who read books, or who couldn't carry tunes, or who used bad language), the ones who always mixed sex and murder and the ones who believed that murder was contaminated by the least breath of sex, the sticklers and the Sloppy Joes, the artists and the butchers, the ax- and stiletto-types, the *com*pulsives and the *re*pulsives—honestly, Pop's portraits from life added up to a Dance of Death as good as anything the Middle Ages ever produced and they ought to have been illustrated like those by some great artist. Pop told us a lot about his own killings too. Alice and me was interested, but neither of us wasn't tempted into making parallel revelations about ourselves. Your private life's your own business, I felt, as close as your guts, and no joke's good enough to justify revealing a knot of it.

Not that we talked about nothing but murder while we were bulleting along toward Atla-Hi. The conversation was free-wheeling and we got onto all sorts of topics. For instance, we got to talking about the plane and how it flew itself—or levitated itself, rather. I said it must generate an antigravity field that was keyed to the body of the plane but nothing else, so that *we* didn't feel lighter, nor any of the objects in the cabin—it just worked on the dull silvery metal—and I proved my point by using Mother to shave a little wisp of metal off the edge of the control board. The curlicue stayed in the air wherever you put it and when you moved it you could feel the faintest sort of gyroscopic resistance. It was very strange.

Pop pointed out it was a little like magnetism. A germ riding on an iron filing that was traveling toward the pole of a big magnet wouldn't feel the magnetic pull—it wouldn't be operating on him, only on the iron—but just the same the germ'd be carried along with the filing and feel its acceleration and all, provided he could hold on—but for that purpose you could imagine a tiny cabin in the filing. "That's what we are," Pop added. "Three germs, jumbo size."

Alice wanted to know why an antigravity plane should have even the stubbiest wings or a jet for that matter, for we remembered now we'd noticed the tubes, and I said it was maybe just a reserve system in case the antigravity failed and Pop guessed it might be for extra-fast battle maneuvering or even for operating outside the atmosphere (which hardly made sense, as I proved to him).

"If we're a battle plane, where's our guns?" Alice asked. None of us had an answer.

We remembered the noise the plane had made before we saw it. It must have been using its jets then. "And do you suppose," Pop asked, "that it was something from the antigravity that made electricity flare out of the top of the cracking plant? Like to have scared the pants off me!" No answer to that either.

Now was a logical time, of course, to ask Pop what he knew about the cracking plant and just who had done the scream if not him, but I figured he still wouldn't talk; as long as we were acting friendly there was no point in spoiling it.

We guessed around a little, though, about where the plane came from. Pop said Alamos, I said Atla-Hi, Alice said why not from both, why couldn't Alamos and Atla-Hi have some sort of treaty and the plane be traveling from the one to the other. We agreed it might be. At least it fitted with the Atla-Hi violet and the Alamos blue being brighter than the other colors.

"I just hope we got some sort of anti-collision radar," I said. I guessed we had, because twice we'd jogged in our course a little, maybe to clear the Alleghenies. The easterly green star was by now getting pretty close to the violet blot of Atla-Hi. I looked out at the orange soup, which was *one* thing that hadn't changed a bit so far, and I got to wishing like a baby that it wasn't there and to thinking how it blanketed the whole Earth (stars over the Riviera?—don't make me laugh!) and I heard myself asking, "Pop, did you rub out that guy that pushed the buttons for all this?"

"Nope," Pop answered without hesitation, just as if it hadn't been four hours or so since he'd mentioned the point. "Nope, Ray. Fact is I welcomed him into our little fellowship about six months back. This is *his* knife here, this horn-handle in my boot, though he never killed with it. He claimed he'd been tortured for years by the thought of the millions and millions he'd killed with blast and radiation, but now he was finding peace at last because he was where he belonged, with the murderers, and could start to do something about it. Several of the boys didn't want to let him in. They claimed he wasn't a real murderer, doing it by remote control, no matter how many he bumped off."

"I'd have been on their side," Alice said, thinning her lips.

"Yep," Pop continued, "they got real hot about it. *He* got hot too and all excited and offered to go out and kill somebody with his bare hands right off, or try to (he's a skinny little runt), if that's what he had to do to join. We argued it over, I pointed out that we let ex-soldiers count the killings they'd done in service, and that we counted poisonings and booby traps and such too—which are remote-control killings in a way—so eventually we let him in. He's doing good work. We're fortunate to have him."

"Do you think he's really the guy who pushed the buttons?" I asked Pop.

"How should I know?" Pop replied. "He claims to be."

I was going to say something about people who faked confessions to get a little easy glory, as compared to the guys who were really guilty and would sooner be chopped up than talk about it, but at that moment a fourth voice started talking in the plane. It seemed to be coming out of the violet patch on the North America screen. That is, it came from the general direction of the screen at any rate and my mind instantly tied it to the violet patch at Atla-Hi. It gave us a fright, I can tell you. Alice grabbed my knee with her pliers (she changed again), harder than she'd intended, I suppose, though I didn't let out a yip—I was too defensively frozen.

The voice was talking a language I didn't understand at all that went up and down the scale like atonal music.

"Sounds like Chinese," Pop whispered, giving me a nudge.

"It *is* Chinese. Mandarin," the screen responded instantly in the purest English—at least that was how I'd describe it. Practically Boston. "Who are you? And where is Grayl? Come in, Grayl."

I knew well enough who Grayl must be—or rather, have been. I looked at Pop and Alice. Pop grinned, maybe a mite feebly this time, I thought, and gave me a look as if to say, "*You* want to handle it?"

I cleared my throat. Then, "We've taken over for Grayl," I said to the screen.

"Oh." The screen hesitated, just barely. Then, "Do any of 'you' speak Mandarin?"

I hardly bothered to look at Pop and Alice. "No," I said.

"Oh." Again a tiny pause. "Is Grayl aboard the plane?"

"No." I said.

"Oh. Incapacitated in some way, I suppose?"

"Yes," I said, grateful for the screen's tactfulness, unintentional or not.

"But you have taken over for him?" the screen pressed.

"Yes," I said, swallowing. I didn't know what I was getting us into, things were moving too fast, but it seemed the merest sense to act cooperative.

"I'm very glad of that," the screen said with something in its tone that made me feel funny—I guess it was sincerity.

Then it said, "Is the—" and hesitated, and started again with "Are the blocks aboard?"

I thought. Alice pointed at the stuff she dumped out of the other seat. I said. "There's a box with a thousand or so one-inch underweight steel cubes in it. Like a child's blocks, but with buttons in them. Alongside a box with a parachute."

"That's what I mean," the screen said and somehow, maybe because whoever was talking was trying to hide it, I caught a note of great relief.

"Look," the screen said, more rapidly now, "I don't know how much you know, but we may have to work very fast. You aren't going to be able to deliver the steel cubes to us directly. In fact you aren't going to be able to land in Atlantic Highlands at all. We're sieged in by planes and ground forces of Savannah Fortress. All our aircraft, such as haven't been destroyed, are pinned down. You're going to have to parachute the blocks to a point as near as possible to one of our ground parties that's made a sortie. We'll give you a signal. I hope it will be later—nearer here, that is—but it may be sooner. Do you know how to fight the plane you're in? Operate its armament?"

"No," I said, wetting my lip.

"Then that's the first thing I'd best teach you. Anything you see in the haze from now on will be from Savannah. You must shoot it down."

CHAPTER FIVE

And we are here as on a darkling plain
Swept with confused alarms of struggle and flight,
Where ignorant armies clash by night.
—Dover Beach,
by Matthew Arnold

I am not going to try to describe point by point all that happened the next half hour because there was too much of it and it involved all three of us, sometimes doing different things at the same time, and although we were told a lot of things, we were seldom if ever told the why of them, and through it all was the constant impression that we were dealing with human beings (I almost left out the "human" and I'm still not absolutely sure whether I shouldn't) of vastly greater scope—and probably intelligence too—than ourselves.

And that was just the *basic* confusion, to give it a name. After a while the situation got more difficult, as I'll try to tell in due course.

To begin with, it was extremely weird to plunge from a rather leisurely confab about a fairy-tale fellowship of non-practicing murderers into a shooting war between a violet blob and a dark red puddle on a shadowy fluorescent map. The voice didn't throw any great shining lights on this topic, because after the first—and perhaps unguarded—revelation, we learned little more of the war between Atla-Hi and Savannah Fortress and nothing of the reasons behind it. Presumably Savannah was the aggressor, reaching out north after the conquest of Birmingham, but even that was just a guess. It is hard to describe how shadowy it all felt to me; there were some minutes while my mind kept mixing up the whole thing with what I'd read long ago about the Civil War: Savannah was Lee, Atla-Hi was Grant, and we had been dropped spang into the middle of the second Battle of the Wilderness.

Apparently the Savannah planes had some sort of needle ray as part of their armament—at any rate I was warned to watch out for "swinging lines in the haze, like straight strings of pink stars" and later told to aim at the sources of such lines. And naturally I guessed that the steel cubes must be some crucial weapon for Atla-Hi, or ammunition for a weapon, or parts for some essential instrument like a giant computer, but the voice ignored my questions on that point and didn't fall into the couple of crude conversational traps I tried to set. We were to drop the cubes when told, that was all. Pop had the box of them closed again and rigged to the parachute—he took over that job because Alice and me were busy with other things when the instructions on that came through—and he was told how to open the door of the plane for the drop (you just held your hand steadily on a point beside the door), but, as I say, that was all.

Naturally it occurred to me that once we had made the drop, Atla-Hi would have no more use for us and might simply let us be destroyed by Savannah or otherwise— perhaps *want* us to be destroyed—so that it might be wisest for us to refuse to make the drop when the signal came and hang onto those myriad steel cubes as our only bargaining point. Still, I could see no advantage to refusing *before* the signal came. I'd have liked to discuss the point with Alice and maybe Pop too, but apparently everything we said, even whispered, could be overheard by Atla-Hi. (We never did determine, incidentally, whether Atla-Hi could *see* into the cabin of the plane also. I don't believe they could, though they sure had it bugged for sound.)

All in all, we found out almost nothing about Atla-Hi. In fact, three witless germs traveling in a cabin in an iron filing wasn't a bad description of us at all. As I often say of my deductive faculties—think—shmink! But Atla-Hi (always meaning, of course, the personality behind the voice from the screen) found out all it wanted about us—and apparently knew a good deal to start with. For one thing, they must have been tracking our plane for some time, because they guessed it was on automatic and that we could reverse its course but nothing else. Though they seemed under the impression that we could reverse its course to Los Alamos, not the cracking plant. Here obviously I did get a nugget of new data, though it was just about the only one. For a moment the voice from the screen got real unguarded— anxious as it asked, "Do you know if it is true that they have stopped dying at Los Alamos, or are they merely broadcasting that to cheer us up?"

I answered, "Oh yes, they're all fine," to that, but I couldn't have made it very convincing, because the next thing I knew the voice was getting me to admit that we'd only boarded the plane somewhere in the Central Deathlands. I even had to describe the cracking plant and freeway and gas tanks—I couldn't think of a lie that mightn't get us into as much trouble as the truth—and the voice said, "Oh, did Grayl stay there?" and I said, "Yes," and braced myself to do some more admitting, or some heavy lying, as the inspiration took me.

But the voice continued to skirt around the question of what exactly had happened to Grayl. I guess they knew well enough we'd bumped him off, but didn't bring it up because they needed our cooperation—they were handling us like children or savages, you see.

One pretty amazing point—Atla-Hi apparently knew something about Pop's fairy-tale fellowship of non-practicing murderers, because when he had to speak up, while he was getting instructions on preparing the stuff for the drop, the voice said, "Excuse me, but you sound like one of those M. A. boys."

Murderers Anonymous, Pop had said some of their boys called their unorganized organization.

"Yep, I am," Pop admitted uncomfortably.

"Well, a word of advice then, or perhaps I only mean gossip," the screen said, for once getting on a side track. "Most of our people do not believe you are serious about it, although you may think that you are. Our skeptics (which includes all but a very few of us) split quite evenly between those who think that the M. A. spirit is a terminal psychotic illusion and those who believe it is an elaborate ruse in preparation for some concerted attack on cities by Deathlanders."

"Can't say that I blame the either of them," was Pop's only comment. "I think I'm nuts myself and a murderer forever." Alice glared at him for that admission, but it seemed to do us no damage. Pop really did seem out of his depth though during this part of our adventure, more out of his depth than even Alice and me—I mean, as if he could only really function in the Deathland with Deathlanders and wanted to get anything else over quickly.

I think one reason Pop was that way was that he was feeling very intensely something I was feeling myself: a sort of sadness and bewilderment that beings as smart as the voice from the screen sounded should still be fighting wars. Murder, as you must know by now, I can understand and sympathize with deeply, but war?—no!

Oh, I can understand cultural queers fighting city squares and even get a kick out of it and whoop 'em on, but these

Atla-Hi and Alamos folk seemed a different sort of cat altogether (though I'd only come to that point of view today)—the kind of cat that ought to have outgrown war or thought its way around it. Maybe Savannah Fortress had simply forced the war on them and they had to defend themselves. I hadn't contacted any Savannans—they might be as blood-simple as the Porterites. Still, I don't know that it's always a good excuse that somebody else forced you into war. That sort of justification can keep on until the end of time. But who's a germ to judge?

A minute later I was feeling doubly like a germ and a very lowly one, because the situation had just got more difficult and depressing too—the thing had happened that I said I'd tell you about in due course.

The voice was just repeating its instructions to Pop on making the drop, when it broke off of a sudden and a second voice came in, a deep voice with a sort of European accent (not Chinese, oddly)—not talking *to* us, I think, but to the first voice and overlooking or not caring that we could hear.

"*Also* tell them," the second voice said, "that we will blow them out of the sky the instant they stop obeying us! If they should hesitate to make the drop or if they should put a finger on the button that reverses their course, then—*pouf!* Such brutes understand only the language of force. *Also* warn them that the blocks are atomic grenades that will blow them out of the sky too if—"

"Dr. Kovalsky, will you permit me to point out—" the first voice interrupted, getting as close to expressing irritation as I imagine it ever allowed itself to do. Then both voices cut off abruptly and the screen was silent for ten seconds or so. I guess the first voice thought it wasn't nice for us to overhear Atla-Hi bickering with itself, even if the second voice didn't give a damn (any more than a farmer would mind the pigs overhearing him squabble with his hired man; of course this guy seemed to overlook that we were killer-pigs, but there wasn't anything we could do in that line just now except get burned up).

When the screen came on again, it was just the first voice talking once more, but it had something to say that was probably the result of a rapid conference and compromise.

"Attention, everyone! I wish to inform you that the plane in which you are traveling can be exploded—melted in the air, rather—if we activate a certain control at this end. We will *not* do so, now or subsequently, if you make the drop when we give the signal and if you remain on your present course until then. Afterwards you will be at liberty to reverse your course and escape as best you may. Let me re-emphasize that when you told me you had taken over for Grayl I accepted that assertion in full faith and still so accept it. Is that all fully understood?"

We all told him "Yes," though I don't imagine we sounded very happy about it, even Pop. However I did get that funny feeling again that the voice was being really sincere—an illusion, I supposed, but still a comforting one.

Now while all these things were going on, believe it or not, and while the plane continued to bullet through the orange haze—which hadn't shown any foreign objects in it so far, thank God, even vultures, let alone "straight strings of pink stars"—I was receiving a cram course in gunnery! (Do you wonder I don't try to tell this part of my story consecutively?)

It turned out that Alice had been brilliantly right about one thing: if you pushed some of the buttons simultaneously in patterns of five they unlocked and you could play on them like organ keys. Two sets of five keys, played properly, would rig out a sight just in front of the viewport and let you aim and fire the plane's main gun in any forward direction. There was a rearward firing gun too, that you aimed by changing over the World Screen to a rear-view TV window, but we didn't get around to mastering that one. In fact, in spite of my special talents it was all I could do to achieve a beginner's control over the main gun, and I wouldn't have managed even that except that Alice, from the thinking she'd been doing about patterns of five, was quick at understanding from the voice's descriptions which buttons were meant. She couldn't work them herself of course, what with her stump and burnt hand, but she could point them out for me.

After twenty minutes of drill I was a gunner of sorts, sprawled in the right-hand kneeling seat and intently scanning the onrushing orange haze which at last was beginning to change toward the bronze of evening. If something showed up in it I'd be able to make a stab at getting a shot in. Not that I knew what my gun fired—the voice wasn't giving away any unnecessary data.

Naturally I had asked why didn't the voice teach me to fly the plane so that I could maneuver in case of attack, and naturally the voice had told me it was out of the question— much too difficult and besides they wanted us on a known course so they could plan better for the drop and recovery. (I think maybe the voice would have given me some hints—and maybe even told me more about the steel cubes too and how much danger we were in from them—if it hadn't been for the second voice, which presumably had issued from a being who was keeping watch to make sure among other things that the first voice didn't get soft-hearted.)

So there I was being a front gunner. Actually a part of me was getting a big bang out of it—from antique Banker's Special to needle cannon (or whatever it was)—but at the same time another part of me was disgusted with the idea of acting like I belonged to a live culture (even a smart, unqueer one) and working in a war (even just so as to get out of it fast), while a third part of me—one that I normally keep down—was very simply horrified.

Pop was back by the door with the box and 'chute, ready to make the drop.

Alice had no duties for the moment, but she'd suddenly started gathering up food cans and packing them in one bag—I couldn't figure out at first what she had in mind. Orderly housewife wouldn't be exactly my description of her occupational personality.

Then of course everything had to happen at once.

The voice said, "Make the drop!"

Alice crossed to Pop and thrust out the bag of cans toward him, writhing her lips in silent "talk" to tell him something. She had a knife in her burnt hand too.

But I didn't have time to do any lip-reading, because just then a glittering pink asterisk showed up in the darkening haze ahead—a whole half dozen straight lines spreading out from a blank central spot, as if a super-fast gigantic spider had laid in the first strands of its web.

Wind whistled as the door of the plane started to open.

I fought to center my sight on the blank central spot, which drifted toward the left.

One of the straight lines grew dazzlingly bright.

I heard Alice whisper fiercely, "Drop *these*!" and the part of my mind that couldn't be applied to gunnery instantly deduced that she'd had some last-minute inspiration about dropping a bunch of cans instead of the steel cubes.

I got the sight centered and held down the firing combo. The thought flashed to me: *it's a city you're firing at, not a plane*, and I flinched.

The dazzlingly pink line dipped down toward me.

Behind me, the sound of a struggle. Alice snarling and Pop giving a grunt.

Then all at once a scream from Alice, a big whoosh of wind, a flash way ahead (where I'd aimed), a spatter of hot metal inside the cabin, a blinding spot in the middle of the

World Screen, a searing beam inches from my neck, an electric shock that lifted me from my seat and ripped at my consciousness!

When I came to (if I really ever was out—seconds later, at most) there were no more pink lines. The haze was just its disgustingly tawny evening self with black spots that were only after-images. The cabin stunk of ozone, but wind funneling through a hole in the one-time World Screen was blowing it out fast enough—Savannah had gotten in one lick, all right. And we were falling, the plane was swinging down like a crippled bird—I could feel it and there was no use kidding myself.

But staring at the control panel wouldn't keep us from crashing if that was in the cards. I looked around and there were Pop and Alice glaring at each other across the closing door. He looked mean. She looked agonized and was pressing her burnt hand into her side with her elbow as if he'd stamped on the hand, maybe. I didn't see any blood though. I didn't see the box and 'chute either, though I did see Alice's bag of groceries. I guessed Pop had made the drop.

Now, it occurred to me, was a bully time for Voice Two to melt the plane—if he hadn't already tried. My first thought had been that the spatter of hot metal had come from the Savannah craft spitting us, but there was no way to be sure.

I looked around at the viewport in time to see rocks and stunted trees jump out of the haze. *Good old Ray*, I thought, *always in at the death*. But just then the plane took a sickening bounce, as if its antigravity had only started to operate within yards of the ground. Another lurching fall and another bounce, less violent. A couple of repetitions of that, each one a little gentler, and then we were sort of bumping along on an even keel with the rocks and such sliding past fast about a hundred feet below, I judged. We'd been spoiled for altitude work, it seemed, but we could still cripple along in some sort of low-power repulsion field.

I looked at the North America screen and the buttons, wondering if I should start us back west again or leave us set on Atla-Hi and see what the hell happened—at the moment I hardly cared what else Savannah did to us. I needn't have wasted the mental energy. The decision was made for me. As I watched, the Atla-Hi button jumped up by itself and the button for the cracking plant went down and there was some extra bumping as we swung around.

Also, the violet patch of Atla-Hi went real dim and the button for it no longer had a violet nimbus. The Los Alamos blue went dull too. The cracking-plant dot glowed a brighter green—that was all.

All except for one thing. As the violet dimmed I thought I heard Voice One very faintly (not as if speaking directly but as if the screen had heard and remembered—not a voice but the fluorescent ghost of one): "Thank you and good luck!"

CHAPTER SIX

Many a man has dated his ruin from some murder or other that perhaps he thought little of at the time.
—Thomas de Quincey

"And a long merry siege to you, sir, and roast rat for Christmas!" I responded, very out loud and rather to my surprise.

"War! How I hate war!"—that was what Pop exploded with. He didn't exactly dance in senile rage—he was still keeping too sharp a watch on Alice—but his voice sounded that way.

"Damn you, Pop!" Alice contributed. "And you too, Ray! We might have pulled something, but you had to go obedience-happy." Then her anger got the better of her grammar, or maybe Pop and me was corrupting it. "Damn the both of you!" she finished.

It didn't make much sense, any of it. We were just cutting loose, I guess, after being scared to say anything for the last half hour.

I said to Alice, "I don't know what you could have pulled, except the chain on us." To Pop I remarked, "You may hate war, but you sure helped that one along. Those grenades you dropped will probably take care of a few hundred Savannans."

"That's what you always say about me, isn't it?" he snapped back. "But I don't suppose I should expect any kinder interpretation of my motives." To Alice he said, "I'm sorry I had to slap your burnt fingers, sister, but you can't say I didn't warn you about my low-down tactics." Then to me again: "I *do* hate war, Ray. It's just murder on a bigger scale, though some of the boys give me an argument there."

"Then why don't you go preach against war in Atla-Hi and Savannah?" Alice demanded, still very hot but not quite so bitter.

"Yeah, Pop, how about it?" I seconded.

"Maybe I should," he said, thoughtful all at once. "They sure need it." Then he grinned. "Hey, how'd this sound: HEAR THE WORLD-FAMOUS MURDERER POP TRUMBULL TALK AGAINST WAR. WEAR YOUR STEEL THROAT PROTECTORS. Pretty good, hey?"

We all laughed at that, grudgingly at first, then with a touch of wholeheartedness. I think we all recognized that things weren't going to be very cheerful from here on in and we'd better not turn up our noses at the feeblest fun.

"I guess I didn't have anything very bright in mind," Alice admitted to me, while to Pop she said, "All right, I forgive you for the present."

"Don't!" Pop said with a shudder. "I hate to think of what happened to the last bugger made the mistake of forgiving me."

We looked around and took stock of our resources. It was time we did. It was getting dark fast, although we were chasing the sun, and there weren't any cabin lights coming on and we sure didn't know of any way of getting any.

We wadded a couple of satchels into the hole in the World Screen without trying to probe it. After a while it got warmer again in the cabin and the air a little less dusty. Presently it started to get too smoky from the cigarettes we were burning, but that came later.

We screwed off the walls the few storage bags we hadn't inspected. They didn't contain nothing of consequence, not even a flashlight.

I had one last go at the buttons, though there weren't any left with nimbuses on them—the darker it got, the clearer that was. Even the Atla-Hi button wouldn't push now that it had lost its violet halo. I tried the gunnery patterns, figuring to put in a little time taking pot shots at any mountains that turned up, but the buttons that had been responding so well a few minutes ago refused to budge. Alice suggested different patterns, but none of them worked. That console was really locked—maybe the shot from Savannah was partly responsible, though Atla-Hi remote-locking things was explanation enough.

"The buggers!" I said. "They didn't have to tie us up *this* tight. Going east we at least had a choice—forward or back. Now we got none."

"Maybe we're just as well off," Pop said. "If Atla-Hi had been able to do anything more for us—that is, if they hadn't been sieged in, I mean—they'd sure as anything have pulled us in. Pull the plane in, I mean, and picked us out of it—with a big pair of tweezers, likely as not. And contrary to your flattering opinion of my preaching (which by the way none of the religious boys in my outfit share—they call me 'that misguided old atheist'), I don't think none of us would go over big at Atla-Hi."

We had to agree with him there. I couldn't imagine Pop or Alice or even me cutting much of a figure (even if we weren't murder-pariahs) with the pack of geniuses that seemed to make up the Atla-Alamos crowd. The Double-A Republics, to give them a name, might have their small-brain types, but somehow I didn't think so. There must be more than one Edison-Einstein, it seemed to me, back of antigravity and all the wonders in this plane and the other things we'd gotten hints of. Also, Grayl had seemed bred for brains as well as size, even if us small mammals had cooked his goose. And none of the modern "countries" had more than a few thousand population yet, I was pretty sure, and that hardly left room for a dumbbell class. Finally, too, I got hold of a memory I'd been reaching for the last hour—how when I was a kid I'd read about some scientists who learned to talk Mandarin just for kicks. I told Alice and Pop.

"And if *that's* the average Atla-Alamoser's idea of mental recreation," I said, "well, you can see what I mean."

"I'll grant you they got a monopoly of brains," Pop agreed. "Not sense, though," he added doggedly.

"Intellectual snobs," was Alice's comment. "I know the type and I detest it." ("You *are* sort of intellectual, aren't you?" Pop told her, which fortunately didn't start a riot.)

Still, I guess all three of us found it fun to chew over a bit the new slant we'd gotten on two (in a way, three) of the great "countries" of the modern world. (And as long as we thought of it as fun, we didn't have to admit the envy and wistfulness that was behind our wisecracks.)

I said, "We've always figured in a general way that Alamos was the remains of a community of scientists and technicians.

Now we know the same's true of the Atla-Hi group. They're the Brookhaven survivors."

"Manhattan Project, don't you mean?" Alice corrected.

"Nope, that was in Colorado Springs," Pop said with finality.

I also pointed out that a community of scientists would educate for technical intelligence, maybe breed for it too. And being a group picked for high I. Q. to begin with, they might make startlingly fast progress. You could easily imagine such folk, unimpeded by the boobs, creating a wonder world in a couple of generations.

"They got their troubles though," Pop reminded me and that led us to speculating about the war we'd dipped into. Savannah Fortress, we knew, was supposed to be based on some big atomic plants on the river down that way, but its culture seemed to have a fiercer ingredient than Atla-Alamos. Before we knew it we were, musing almost romantically about the plight of Atla-Hi, besieged by superior and (it was easy to suppose) barbaric forces, and maybe distant Los Alamos in a similar predicament—Alice reminded me how the voice had asked if they were still dying out there. For a moment I found myself fiercely proud that I had been able to strike a blow against evil aggressors. At once, of course, then, the revulsion came.

"This is a hell of a way," I said, "for three so-called realists to be mooning about things."

"Yes, especially when your heroes kicked us out," Alice agreed.

Pop chuckled. "Yep," he said, "they even took Ray's artillery away from him."

"You're wrong there, Pop," I said, sitting up. "I still got one of the grenades—the one the pilot had in his fist." To tell the truth I'd forgotten all about it and it bothered me a little now to feel it snugged up in my pocket against my hip bone where the skin is thin.

"You believe what that old Dutchman said about the steel cubes being atomic grenades?" Pop asked me.

"I don't know," I said, "He sure didn't sound enthusiastic about telling us the truth about anything. But for that matter he sounded mean enough to tell the truth figuring we'd think it was a lie. Maybe this *is* some sort of baby A-bomb with a fuse timed like a grenade." I got it out and hefted it. "How about I press the button and drop it out the door? Then we'll know." I really felt like doing it—restless, I guess.

"Don't be a fool, Ray," Alice said.

"Don't tense up, I won't," I told her. At the same time I made myself the little promise that if I ever got to feeling restless, that is, restless and *bad*, I'd just go ahead and punch the button and see what happened—sort of leave my future up to the gods of the Deathlands, you might say.

"What makes you so sure it's a weapon?" Pop asked.

"What else would it be," I asked him, "that they'd be so hot on getting them in the middle of a war?"

"I don't know for sure," Pop said. "I've made a guess, but I don't want to tell it now. What I'm getting at, Ray, is that your first thought about anything you find—in the world outside or in your own mind—is that it's a weapon."

"Anything worthwhile in your mind is a weapon!" Alice interjected with surprising intensity.

"You see?" Pop said. "That's what I mean about the both of you. That sort of thinking's been going on a long time. Cave man picks up a rock and right away asks himself, 'Who can I brain with this?' Doesn't occur to him for several hundred thousand years to use it to start building a hospital."

"You know, Pop," I said, carefully tucking the cube back in my pocket, "you *are* sort of preachy at times."

"Guess I am," he said. "How about some grub?"

It was a good idea. Another few minutes and we wouldn't have been able to see to eat, though with the cans shaped to tell their contents I guess we'd have managed. It was a funny circumstance that in this wonder plane we didn't even know how to turn on the light—and a good measure of our general helplessness.

We had our little feed and lit up again and settled ourselves. I judged it would be an overnight trip, at least to the cracking plant—we weren't making anything like the speed we had been going east. Pop was sitting in back again and Alice and I lay half hitched around on the kneeling seats, which allowed us to watch each other. Pretty soon it got so dark we couldn't see anything of each other but the glowing tips of the cigarettes and a bit of face around the mouth when the person took a deep drag. They were a good idea, those cigarettes—kept us from having ideas about the other person starting to creep around with a knife in his hand.

The North America screen still glowed dimly and we could watch our green dot trying to make progress. The viewport was dead black at first, then there came the faintest sort of bronze blotch that very slowly shifted forward and down. The Old Moon, of course, going west ahead of us.

After a while I realized what it was like—an old Pullman car (I'd traveled in one once as a kid) or especially the smoker of an old Pullman, very late at night. Our crippled antigravity, working on the irregularities of the ground as they came along below, made the ride rhythmically bumpy, you see. I remembered how lonely and strange that old sleeping car had seemed to me as a kid. This felt the same. I kept waiting for a hoot or a whistle. It was the sort of loneliness that settles in your bones and keeps working at you.

"I recall the first man I ever killed—" Pop started to reminisce softly.

"Shut up!" Alice told him. "Don't you ever talk about anything but murder, Pop?"

"Guess not," he said. "After all, it's the only really interesting topic there is. Do you know of another?"

It was silent in the cabin for a long time after that. Then Alice said, "It was the afternoon before my twelfth birthday when they came into the kitchen and killed my father. He'd been wise, in a way, and had us living at a spot where the bombs didn't touch us or the worst fallout. But he hadn't counted on the local werewolf gang. He'd just been slicing some bread—homemade from our own wheat (Dad was great on back to nature and all)—but he laid down the knife.

"Dad couldn't see any object or idea as a weapon, you see—that was his great weakness. Dad couldn't even see weapons as weapons. Dad had a philosophy of cooperation, that was his name for it, that he was going to explain to people. Sometimes I think he was glad of the Last War, because he believed it would give him his chance.

"But the werewolves weren't interested in philosophy and although their knives weren't as sharp as Dad's they didn't lay them down. Afterwards they had themselves a meal, with me for dessert. I remember one of them used a slice of bread to sop up blood like gravy. And another washed his hands and face in the cold coffee..."

She didn't say anything else for a bit. Pop said softly, "That was the afternoon, wasn't it, that the fallen angels..." and then just said, "My big mouth."

"You were going to say 'the afternoon they killed God?'" Alice asked him. "You're right, it was. They killed God in the kitchen that afternoon. That's how I know he's dead. Afterwards they would have killed me too, eventually, except—"

Aain she broke off, this time to say, "Pop, do you suppose I can have been thinking about myself as the Daughter of

God all these years? That that's why everything seems so intense?"

"I don't know," Pop said. "The religious boys say we're all children of God. I don't put much stock in it—or else God sure has some lousy children. Go on with your story."

"Well, they would have killed me too, except the leader took a fancy to me and got the idea of training me up for a Weregirl or She-wolf Deb or whatever they called it."

"That was my first experience of ideas as weapons. He got an idea about me and I used it to kill him. I had to wait three months for my opportunity. I got him so lazy he let me shave him. He bled to death the same way as Dad."

"Hum," Pop commented after a bit, "that was a chiller, all right. I got to remember to tell it to Bill—it was somebody killing his mother that got *him* started. Alice, you had about as good a justification for your first murder as any I remember hearing."

"Yet," Alice said after another pause, with just a trace of the old sarcasm creeping back into her voice, "I don't suppose you think I was right to do it?"

"Right? Wrong? Who knows?" Pop said almost blusteringly. "Sure you were justified in a whole pack of ways. Anybody'd sympathize with you. A man often has fine justification for the first murder he commits. But as you must know, it's not that the first murder's always so bad in itself as that it's apt to start you on a killing spree. Your sense of values gets shifted a tiny bit and never shifts back. But you know all that and who am I to tell you anything, anyway? I've killed men because I didn't like the way they spit. And may very well do it again if I don't keep watching myself and my mind ventilated."

"Well, Pop," Alice said, "I didn't always have such dandy justification for my killings. Last one was a moony old physicist—he fixed me the Geiger counter I carry. A silly old geek—I don't know how he survived so long. Maybe an exile or a runaway. You know, I often attach myself to the elderly do-gooder type like my father was. Or like you, Pop."

Pop nodded. "It's good to know yourself," he said.

There was a third pause and then, although I hadn't exactly been intending to, I said, "Alice had justification for her first murder, personal justification that an ape would understand. I had no personal justification at all for mine, yet I killed about a million people at a modest estimate. You see, I was the boss of the crew that took care of the hydrogen missile ticketed for Moscow, and when the ticket was finally taken up I was the one to punch it. My finger on the firing button, I mean."

I went on, "Yeah, Pop, I was one of the button-pushers. There were really quite a few of us, of course—that's why I get such a laugh out of stories about being or rubbing out the *one* guy who pushed all the buttons."

"That so?" Pop said with only mild-sounding interest. "In that case you ought to know—"

We didn't get to hear right then who I ought to know because I had a fit of coughing and we realized the cigarette smoke was getting just too thick. Pop fixed the door so it was open a crack and after a while the atmosphere got reasonably okay though we had to put up with a low lonely whistling sound.

"Yeah," I continued, "I was the boss of the missile crew and I wore a very handsome uniform with impressive insignia—not the bully old stripes I got on my chest now— and I was very young and handsome myself. We were all very young in that line of service, though a few of the men under me were a little older. Young and dedicated. I remember feeling a very deep and grim—and *clean*—responsibility. But I wonder sometimes just how deep it went or how clean it really was.

"I had an uncle flew in the war they fought to lick fascism, bombardier on a Flying Fortress or something, and once when he got drunk he told me how some days it didn't bother him at all to drop the eggs on Germany; the buildings and people down there seemed just like toys that a kid sets up to kick over, and the whole business about as naive fun as poking an anthill.

"*I* didn't even have to fly over at seven miles what I was going to be aiming at. Only I remember sometimes getting out a map and looking at a certain large dot on it and smiling a little and softly saying, 'Pow!'—and then giving a little conventional shudder and folding up the map quick.

"Naturally we told ourselves we'd never have to do it, fire the thing, I mean, we joked about how after twenty years or so we'd all be given jobs as museum attendants of this same bomb, deactivated at last. But naturally it didn't work out that way. There came the day when our side of the world got hit and the orders started cascading down from Defense Coordinator Bigelow—"

"Bigelow?" Pop interrupted. "Not Joe Bigelow?"

"Joseph A., I believe," I told him, a little annoyed.

"Why he's my boy then, the one I was telling you about—the skinny runt had this horn-handle! Can you beat that?" Pop sounded startlingly happy. "Him and you'll have a lot to talk about when you get together."

I wasn't so sure of that myself, in fact my first reaction was that the opposite would be true. To be honest I was for the first moment more than a little annoyed at Pop interrupting my story of my Big Grief—for it was that to me, make no mistake. Here my story had finally been teased out of me, against all expectation, after decades of repression and in spite of dozens of assorted psychological blocks—and here was Pop interrupting it for the sake of a lot of trivial organizational gossip about Joes and Bills and Georges we'd never heard of and what they'd say or think!

But then all of a sudden I realized that I didn't really care, that it didn't feel like a Big Grief any more, that just starting to tell about it after hearing Pop and Alice tell their stories had purged it of that unnecessary weight of feeling that had made it a millstone around my neck. It seemed to me now that I could look down at Ray Baker from a considerable height (but not an angelic or contemptuously superior height) and ask myself *not* why he had grieved so much—that was understandable and even desirable—but why he had grieved so *uselessly* in such a stuffy little private hell.

And it *would* be interesting to find out how Joseph A. Bigelow had felt.

"How does it feel, Ray, to kill a million people?"

I realized that Alice had asked me the question several seconds back and it was hanging in the air.

"That's just what I've been trying to tell you," I told her and started to explain it all over again—the words poured out of me now. I won't put them down here—it would take too long—but they were honest words as far as I knew and they eased me.

I couldn't get over it: here were us three murderers feeling a trust and understanding and sharing a communion that I wouldn't have believed possible between *any* two or three people in the Age of the Deaders—or in *any* age, to tell the truth. It was against everything I knew of Deathland psychology, but it was happening just the same. Oh, our strange isolation had something to do with it, I knew, and that Pullman-car memory hypnotizing my mind, and our reactions to the voices and violence of Atla-Alamos, but in spite of all that I ranked it as a wonder. I felt an inward freedom and easiness that I never would have believed possible. Pop's little disorganized organization had really got hold of something, I couldn't deny it.

Three treacherous killers talking from the bottoms of their hearts and believing each other!—for it never occurred to me to doubt that Pop and Alice were feeling exactly like I was. In fact, we were all so sure of it that we didn't even mention our communion to each other. Perhaps we were a little afraid we would rub off the bloom. We just enjoyed it.

We must have talked about a thousand things that night and smoked a couple of hundred cigarettes. After a while we started taking little catnaps—we'd gotten too much off our chests and come to feel too tranquil for even our excitement to keep us awake. I remember the first time I dozed waking up with a cold start and grabbing for Mother—and then hearing Pop and Alice gabbing in the dark, and remembering what had happened, and relaxing again with a smile.

Of all things, Pop was saying, "Yep, I imagine Ray must be good to make love to, murderers almost always are, they got the fire. It reminds me of what a guy named Fred told me, one of our boys..."

Mostly we took turns going to sleep, though I think there were times when all three of us were snoozing. About the fifth time I woke up, after some tighter shut-eye, the orange soup was back again outside and Alice was snoring gently in the next seat and Pop was up and had one of his knives out.

He was looking at his reflection in the viewport. His face gleamed. He was rubbing butter into it.

"Another day, another pack of troubles," he said cheerfully.

The tone of his remark jangled my nerves, as that tone generally does early in the morning. I squeezed my eyes. "Where are we?" I asked.

He poked his elbow toward the North America screen. The two green dots were almost one.

"My God, we're practically there," Alice said for me. She'd waked fast, Deathlands style.

"I know," Pop said, concentrating on what he was doing, "but I aim to be shaved before they commence landing maneuvers."

"You think automatic will land us?" Alice asked. "What if we just start circling around?"

"We can figure out what to do when it happens," Pop said, whittling away at his chin. "Until then, I'm not interested. There's still a couple of bottles of coffee in the sack. I've had mine."

I didn't join in this chit-chat because the green dots and Alice's first remark had reminded me of a lot deeper reason for my jangled nerves than Pop's cheerfulness. Night was gone, with its shielding cloak and its feeling of being able to talk forever, and the naked day was here, with its demands for action. It is not so difficult to change your whole view of life when you are flying, or even bumping along above the ground with friends who understand, but soon, I knew, I'd be down in the dust with something I never wanted to see again.

"Coffee, Ray?"

"Yeah, I guess so." I took the bottle from Alice and wondered whether my face looked as glum as hers.

"They shouldn't salt butter," Pop asserted. "It makes it lousy for shaving."

"It was the *best* butter," Alice said.

"Yeah," I said. "The Dormouse, when they buttered the watch."

It may be true that feeble humor is better than none. I don't know.

"What are you two yakking about?" Pop demanded.

"A book we both read," I told him.

"Either of you writers?" Pop asked with sudden interest. "Some of the boys think we should have a book about us. I say it's too soon, but they say we might all die off or something. Whoa, Jenny! Easy does it. Gently, please!"

That last remark was by way of recognizing that the plane had started an authoritative turn to the left. I got a sick and cold feeling. This was it.

Pop sheathed his knife and gave his face a final rub. Alice belted on her satchel. I reached for my knapsack, but I was staring through the viewport, dead ahead.

The haze lightened faintly, three times. I remembered the St. Elmo's fire that had flamed from the cracking plant.

"Pop," I said—almost whined, to be truthful, "why'd the bugger ever have to land here in the first place? He was rushing stuff they needed bad at Atla-Hi—why'd he have to break his trip?"

"That's easy," Pop said. "He was being a bad boy. At least that's my theory. He was supposed to go straight to Atla-Hi, but there was somebody he wanted to check up on first. He stopped here to see his girlfriend. Yep, his girlfriend. She tried to warn him off—that's my explanation of the juice that flared out of the cracking plant and interfered with his landing, though I'm sure she didn't intend the last. By the way, whatever she turned on to give him the warning must still be turned on. But Grayl came on down in spite of it."

Before I could assimilate that, the seven deformed gas tanks materialized in the haze. We got the freeway in our sights and steadied and slowed and kept slowing. The plane didn't graze the cracking plant this time, though I'd have sworn it was going to hit it head on. When I saw we *weren't* going to hit it, I wanted to shut my eyes, but I couldn't.

The stain was black now and the Pilot's body was thicker than I remembered—bloated. But that wouldn't last long. Three or four vultures were working on it.

CHAPTER SEVEN

Here now in his triumph where all things falter,
Stretched out on the spoils that his own hand spread,
As a god self-slain on his own strange altar,
Death lies dead.
—A Forsaken Garden,
by Charles Swinburne

Pop was first down. Between us we helped Alice. Before joining them I took a last look at the control panel. The cracking plant button was up again and there was a blue nimbus on another button. For Los Alamos, I supposed. I was tempted to push it and get away solo, but then I thought, *nope, there's nothing for me at the other end and the loneliness will be worse than what I got to face here.* I climbed out.

I didn't look at the body, although we were practically on top of it. I saw a little patch of silver off to one side and remembered the gun that had melted. The vultures had waddled off but only a few yards.

"We could kill them," Alice said to Pop.

"Why?" he responded. "Didn't some Hindus use them to take care of dead bodies? Not a bad idea, either."

"Parsees," Alice amplified.

"Yep, Parsees, that's what I meant. Give you a nice clean skeleton in a matter of days."

Pop was leading us past the body toward the cracking plant. I heard the flies buzzing loudly. I felt terrible. I wanted to be dead myself. Just walking along after Pop was an awful effort.

"His girl was running a hidden observation tower here," Pop was saying now. "Weather and all that, I suppose. Or maybe setting up a robot station of some kind. I couldn't tell you about her before, because you were both in a mood to try to rub out anybody remotely connected with the Pilot. In fact, I did my best to lead you astray, letting you think I'd been the one to scream and all. Even now, to be honest about it, I don't know if I'm doing the right thing telling and showing you all this, but a man's got to take some risks whatever he does."

"Say, Pop," I said dully, "isn't she apt to take a shot at us or something?" Not that I'd have minded on my own account. "Or are you and her that good friends?"

"Nope, Ray," he said, "she doesn't even know me. But I don't think she's in a position to do any shooting. You'll see why. Hey, she hasn't even shut the door. That's bad."

He seemed to be referring to a kind of manhole cover standing on its edge just inside the open-walled first story of the cracking plant. He knelt and looked down the hole the cover was designed to close off.

"Well, at least she didn't collapse at the bottom of the shaft," he said. "Come on, let's see what happened." And he climbed into the shaft.

We followed him like zombies. At least that's how I felt. The shaft was about twenty feet deep. There were foot- and hand-holds. It got stuffy right away, and warmer, in spite of the shaft being open at the top.

At the bottom there was a short horizontal passage. We had to duck to get through it. When we could straighten up we were in a large and luxurious bomb-resistant dugout, to give it a name. And it was stuffier and hotter than ever.

There was a lot of scientific equipment around and several small control panels reminding me of the one in the back of the plane. Some of them, I supposed, connected with instruments, weather and otherwise, hidden up in the skeletal structure of the cracking plant. And there were signs of occupancy, a young woman's occupancy—clothes scattered around in a frivolous way, and some small objects of art, and a slightly more than life-size head in clay that I guessed the occupant must have been sculpting. I didn't give that last more than the most fleeting look, strictly unintentional to begin with, because although it wasn't finished I could tell whose head it was supposed to be—the Pilot's.

The whole place was finished in dull silver like the cabin of the plane, and likewise it instantly struck me as having a living personality, partly the Pilot's and partly someone else's—the personality of a marriage. Which wasn't a bit nice, because the whole place smelt of death.

But to tell the truth I didn't give the place more than the quickest look-over, because my attention was rivetted almost at once on a long wide couch with the covers kicked off it and on the body there.

The woman was about six feet tall and built like a goddess. Her hair was blonde and her skin tanned. She was lying on her stomach and she was naked.

She didn't come anywhere near my libido, though. She looked sick to death. Her face, twisted towards us, was hollow-cheeked and flushed. Her eyes, closed, were sunken and dark-circled. She was breathing shallowly and rapidly through her open mouth, gasping now and then.

I got the crazy impression that all the heat in the place was coming from her body, radiating from her fever.

And the whole place stunk of death. Honestly it seemed to me that this dugout was Death's underground temple, the bed Death's altar, and the woman Death's sacrifice. (Had I unconsciously come to worship Death as a god in the Deathlands? I don't really know. There it gets too deep for me.)

No, she didn't come within a million miles of my libido, but there was another part of me that she was eating at...

If guilt's a luxury, then I'm a plutocrat.

...eating at until I was an empty shell, until I had no props left, until I wanted to die then and there, until I figured I had to die...

There was a faint sharp hiss right at my elbow. I looked and found that, unbeknownst to myself, I'd taken the steel cube out of my pocket and holding it snuggled between my first and second fingers I'd punched the button with my thumb just as I'd promised myself I would if I got to really feeling bad.

It goes to show you that you should never give your mind any kind of instructions even half in fun, unless you're prepared to have them carried out whether you approve later or not.

Pop saw what I'd done and looked at me strangely. "So you had to die after all, Ray," he said softly. "Most of us find out we have to, one way or another."

We waited. Nothing happened. I noticed a very faint milky cloud a few inches across hanging in the air by the cube.

Thinking right away of poison gas, I jerked away a little, dispersing the cloud.

"What's that?" I demanded of no one in particular.

"I'd say," said Pop, "that that's something that squirted out of a tiny hole in the side of the cube opposite the button. A hole so nearly microscopic you wouldn't see it unless you looked for it hard. Ray, I don't think you're going to get your baby A-blast, and what's more I'm afraid you've wasted something that's damn valuable. But don't let it worry you. Before I dropped those cubes for Atla-Hi I snagged one."

And darn if he didn't pull the brother of my cube out of his pocket.

"Alice," he said, "I noticed a half pint of whiskey in your satchel when we got the salve. Would you put some on a rag and hand it to me."

Alice looked at him like he was nuts, but while her eyes were looking her pliers and her gloved hand were doing what he told her.

Pop took the rag and swabbed a spot on the sick woman's nearest buttock and jammed the cube against the spot and pushed the button.

"It's a jet hypodermic, folks," he said.

He took the cube away and there was the welt to substantiate his statement.

"Hope we got to her in time," he said. "The plague is tough. Now I guess there's nothing for us to do but wait, maybe for quite a while."

I felt shaken beyond all recognition.

Pop, you old caveman detective!" I burst out. "When did you get that idea for a steel hospital?" Don't think I was feeling anywhere near that gay. It was reaction, close to hysterical.

Pop was taken aback, but then he grinned. "I had a couple of clues that you and Alice didn't," he said. "I knew there was a very sick woman involved. And I had that bout with Los Alamos fever I told you. They've had a lot of trouble with it, I believe—some say its spores come from outside the world with the cosmic dust—and now it seems to have been carried to Atla-Hi. Let's hope they've found the answer this time. Alice, maybe we'd better start getting some water into this gal."

After a while we sat down and fitted the facts together more orderly. Pop did the fitting mostly. Alamos researchers must have been working for years on the plague as it ravaged intermittently, maybe with mutations and ET tricks to make the job harder. Very recently they'd found a promising treatment (cure, we hoped) and prepared it for rush shipment to Atla-Hi, where the plague was raging too and they were sieged in by Savannah as well. Grayl was picked to fly the serum, or drug or whatever it was. But he knew or guessed that this lone woman observer (because she'd fallen out of radio communication or something) had come down with the plague too and he decided to land some serum for her, probably without authorization.

"How do we know she's his girlfriend?" I asked.

"Or wife," Pop said tolerantly. "Why, there was that bag of woman's stuff he was carrying, frilly things like a man would bring for a woman. Who else'd he be apt to make a special stop for?

"Another thing," Pop said. "He must have been using jets to hurry his trip. We heard them, you know."

That seemed about as close a reconstruction of events as we could get. Strictly hypothetical, of course. Deathlanders trying to figure out what goes on inside a "country" like Atla-Alamos and *why* are sort of like foxes trying to understand world politics, or wolves the Gothic migrations. Of course we're all human beings, but that doesn't mean as much as it sounds.

Then Pop told us how he'd happened to be on the scene. He'd been doing a "tour of duty", as he called it, when he spotted this woman's observatory and decided to hang around anonymously and watch over her for a few days and maybe help protect her from some dangerous characters that he knew were in the neighborhood.

"Pop, that sounds like a lousy idea to me," I objected. "Risky, I mean. Spying on another person, watching them without their knowing, would be the surest way to stir up in me the idea of murdering them. Safest thing for me to do in that situation would be to turn around and run."

"*You* probably should," he agreed. "For now, anyway. It's all a matter of knowing your own strength and stage of growth. Me, it helps to give myself these little jobs. And the essence of 'em is that the other person shouldn't know I'm helping."

It sounded like knighthood and pilgrimage and the Boy Scouts all over again—for murderers. Well, why not?

Pop had seen this woman come out of the manhole a couple of times and look around and then go back down and he'd got the impression she was sick and troubled. He'd even guessed she might be coming down with Alamos fever. He'd seen us arrive, of course, and that had bothered him. Then when the plane landed she'd come up again, acting out of her head, but when she'd seen the Pilot and us going for him she'd given that scream and collapsed at the top of the shaft. He'd figured the only thing he could do for her was keep us occupied. Besides, now that he knew for sure we were murderers he'd started to burn with the desire to talk to us and maybe help us quit killing if we seemed to want to. It was only much later, in the middle of our trip, that he began to suspect that the steel cubes were jet hypodermics.

While Pop had been telling us all this, we hadn't been watching the woman so closely. Now Alice called our attention to her. Her skin was covered with fine beads of perspiration, like diamonds.

"That's a good sign," Pop said and Alice started to wipe her off. While she was doing that the woman came to in a groggy sort of way and Pop fed her some thin soup and in the middle of his doing it she dropped off to sleep.

Alice said, "Any other time I would be wild to kill another woman that beautiful. But she has been so close to death that I would feel I was robbing another murderer. I suppose there is more behind the change in my feelings than that, though."

"Yeah, a little, I suppose," Pop said.

I didn't have anything to say about my own feelings. Certainly not out loud. I knew that they had changed and that they were still changing. It was complicated.

After a while it occurred to me and Alice to worry whether we mightn't catch this woman's sickness. It would serve us right, of course, but plague is plague. But Pop reassured us. "Actually I snagged three cubes," he said. "That should take care of you two. I figure I'm immune."

Time wore on. Pop dragged out the harmonica, as I'd been afraid he would, but his playing wasn't too bad. "Tenting Tonight," "When Johnnie Comes Marching Home," and such. We had a meal.

The Pilot's woman woke up again, in her full mind this time or something like it. We were clustered around the bed, smiling a little I suppose and looking inquiring. Being even assistant nurses makes you all concerned about the patient's health and state of mind.

Pop helped her sit up a little. She looked around. She saw me and Alice. Recognition came into her eyes. She drew away from us with a look of loathing. She didn't say a word, but the look stayed.

Pop drew me aside and whispered, "I think it would be a nice gesture if you and Alice took a blanket and went up and sewed him into it. I noticed a big needle and some thread in her satchel." He looked me in the eye and added, "You can't expect this woman to feel any other way toward you, you know. Now or ever."

He was right of course. I gave Alice the high sign and we got out.

No point in dwelling on the next scene. Alice and me sewed up in a blanket a big guy who'd been dead a day and worked over by vultures. That's all.

About the time we'd finished, Pop came up.

"She chased me out," he explained. "She's getting dressed. When I told her about the plane, she said she was going back to Los Alamos. She's not fit to travel, of course, but she's giving herself injections. It's none of our business. Incidentally, she wants to take the body back with her. I told her how we'd dropped the serum and how you and Alice had helped and she listened."

The Pilot's woman wasn't long after Pop. She must have had trouble getting up the shaft, she had a little trouble even walking straight, but she held her head high. She was wearing a dull silver tunic and sandals and cloak. As she passed me and Alice I could see the look of loathing come back into her eyes, and her chin went a little higher. I thought, why shouldn't she want us dead? Right now she probably wants to be dead herself.

Pop nodded to us and we hoisted up the body and followed her. It was almost too heavy a load even for the three of us.

As she reached the plane a silver ladder telescoped down to her from below the door. I thought, *the Pilot must have had it keyed to her some way, so it would let down for her but nobody else. A very lovely gesture.*

The ladder went up after her and we managed to lift the body above our heads, our arms straight, and we walked it through the door of the plane that way, she receiving it.

The door closed and we stood back and the plane took off into the orange haze, us watching it until it was swallowed.

Pop said, "Right now, I imagine you two feel pretty good in a screwed-up sort of way. I know I do. But take it from me, it won't last. A day or two and we're going to start feeling another way, the *old* way, if we don't get busy."

I knew he was right. You don't shake Old Urge Number One anything like that easy.

"So," said Pop, "I got places I want to show you. Guys I want you to meet. And there's things to do, a lot of them. Let's get moving."

So there's my story. Alice is still with me (Urge Number Two is even harder to shake, supposing you wanted to) and we haven't killed anybody lately. (Not since the Pilot, in fact, but it doesn't do to boast.) We're making a stab (my language!) at doing the sort of work Pop does in the Deathlands. It's tough but interesting. I still carry a knife, but I've given Mother to Pop. He has it strapped to him alongside Alice's screw-in blade.

Atla-Hi and Alamos still seem to be in existence, so I guess the serum worked for them generally as it did for the Pilot's Woman; they haven't sent us any medals, but they haven't sent a hangman's squad after us either—which is more than fair, you'll admit. But Savannah, turned back from Atla-Hi, is still going strong: there's a rumor they have an army at the gates of Ouachita right now. We tell Pop he'd better start preaching fast—it's one of our standard jokes.

There's also a rumor that a certain fellowship of Deathlanders is doing surprisingly well, a rumor that there's a new America growing in the Deathlands—an America that never need kill again. But don't put too much stock in it. Not *too* much.

THE END

If you've enjoyed this book, you will not want to miss these terrific titles…

ARMCHAIR SCI-FI & HORROR DOUBLE NOVELS, $12.95 each

D-71 **THE DEEP END** by Gregory Luce
TO WATCH BY NIGHT by Robert Moore Williams

D-72 **SWORDSMAN OF LOST TERRA** by Poul Anderson
PLANET OF GHOSTS by David V. Reed

D-73 **MOON OF BATTLE** by J. J. Allerton
THE MUTANT WEAPON by Murray Leinster

D-74 **OLD SPACEMEN NEVER DIE!** John Jakes
RETURN TO EARTH by Bryan Berry

D-75 **THE THING FROM UNDERNEATH** by Milton Lesser
OPERATION INTERSTELLAR by George O. Smith

D-76 **THE BURNING WORLD** by Algis Budrys
FOREVER IS TOO LONG by Chester S. Geier

D-77 **THE COSMIC JUNKMAN** by Rog Phillips
THE ULTIMATE WEAPON by John W. Campbell

D-78 **THE TIES OF EARTH** by James H. Schmitz
CUE FOR QUIET by Thomas L. Sherred

D-79 **SECRET OF THE MARTIANS** by Paul W. Fairman
THE VARIABLE MAN by Philip K. Dick

D-80 **THE GREEN GIRL** by Jack Williamson
THE ROBOT PERIL by Don Wilcox

ARMCHAIR SCIENCE FICTION CLASSICS, $12.95 each

C-25 **THE STAR KINGS**
b   y Edmond Hamilton

C-26 **NOT IN SOLITUDE**
by Kenneth Gantz

C-32 **PROMETHEUS II**
by S. J. Byrne

ARMCHAIR SCIENCE FICTION & HORROR GEMS SERIES, $12.95 each

G-7 **SCIENCE FICTION GEMS, Vol. Seven**
Jack Sharkey and others

G-8 **HORROR GEMS, Vol. Eight**
Seabury Quinn and others